Kayla's Secret

Reba novels by Marian Flandrick Bray

A REBA 3 NOVEL

Kayla's Secret

Marian Flandrick Bray

ZondervanPublishingHouse

Grand Rapids, Michigan

A Division of HarperCollinsPublishers

Kayla's Secret
Copyright © 1996 by Marian Bray

Requests for information should be addressed to:

📖ZondervanPublishingHouse
Grand Rapids, Michigan 49530

Library of Congress Cataloging-in-Publication Data

Bray, Marian Flandrick, 1957– .
    Kayla's secret / Marian Flandrick Bray.
       p.   cm.—(Reba novel ; 3)
    Summary: Having Burrito with her helps sixth-grader Reba adjust to life in
the city where her new friends live dangerously and where Kayla hides in a
makeshift shelter.
    ISBN: 0-310-43351-7 (pbk.)
    [1. Child abuse—Fiction. 2. Friendship—Fiction. 3. Donkeys—Fiction.]
I. Title. II. Series: Bray, Marian Flandrick, 1957– Reba novel ; 3.
PZ7.B7388Kay   1996
[Fic]—dc 20   96–11943
                                              CIP
                                              AC

Printed in the United States of America

96 97 98 99 00 01 02 /❖ DH/ 10 9 8 7 6 5 4 3 2 1

To Heather M.
who gave us her Kayla

Contents

*"If men had wings and bore black feathers,
few of them would be clever enough to be crows."*

—*Henry Ward Beecher, preacher and brother
to Harriet Beecher Stowe of* Uncle Tom's Cabin

1

Crazy in the City

If I had to clean one more counter or wipe down one more baseboard, I'd go crazy. I would. I really would.

"Can I go?" I asked, on the verge of whining. "Now?" Actually I *was* whining. The craziness was real.

Silence answered me. I peeked out of the bathroom around the corner of the living room. Mama and Francisco, my new stepfather, stood, arms around each other, before the window facing the street.

A street! We'd never lived in a house that faced a street before. We'd always had a view of the San

Gabriel Mountains, rising ever higher to the north, like the belly and angled legs of brown, rearing horses.

Mama turned her head, saw me, nodded slightly without a noise, then moved closer to Francisco, as if that were even possible. I had to get away from here.

I thrust my skateboard under my arm and shot across the living room, which was still strewn with unpacked cardboard boxes.

The door chirped as I threw it open and fled. My feet sprang over the front dirt. The grass had been gone a long time. Only a drooping Chinese elm tree hunched over the yard like an old man hunting for lost coins. The elm had scattered tiny leaves over the dirt, and the long branches dangled like fingertips, searching for them.

Our rental house was thrashed, and this was not just my opinion. Miguel, my second oldest brother, had declared it a house fit for crack dealers. As if he knew. I'm sure it wasn't that bad. Francisco said the owners would take off part of the rent if we fixed up things like the lawn and the backyard, which was mostly weeds. He and Mama were saving for a down payment on a condo, which sounded even worse than a crack dealer's house.

I was used to living in open space, only the mountains and sky around me. Now cars, like big red ants, moved around tall buildings, and airplanes buzzed over like flies.

Could we plant a garden in the front dirt? Tangles of wild mountain flowers—would they grow here? Some carrots for Burrito, my pet burro, who by a sheer miracle came with me to the city. Maybe God did care about me.

I put my skateboard down, kicked off, and bumped down the street. Andres, my youngest brother, was two doors down turning somersaults on a real grass lawn with a couple of kids. I waved.

He looked up, with his small, oval face and goofy grin, and waved back.

The skateboard wheels rumbled down the uneven street. When the asphalt ended, I jumped off my board, snatched it up, and walked along the short dirt road that curved behind several houses with big yards, left over from Santa Ana's rural time more than thirty years ago.

At the end of the dirt road, an open, sagging chain link gate beckoned me into the stable, which was smaller than our mountain packing station's barn and pastures. Of course, this was a citified stable.

Citified. My whole world had changed from brown and gold mountains to gray and black exhaust and city streets. Would I stay the same here? Wouldn't a landscape alter someone, especially if it was a totally alien landscape?

I didn't want to be a cramped, crazy city person. I just wouldn't let the landscape alter me, I decided. I'd resist, like a stubborn donkey. I shook my fist at the seven foot cement wall on one side of the dirt road.

"You can't change me," I informed it.

A crow appeared from a palm tree and cawed. Then I held up my arms. Crows lived in the mountains, too.

Two elderly barking dogs ran from the barn toward me, dust pluming behind them like afterburn.

"Hi, Butch, hi, Sheba," I greeted them. No use resisting city dogs. They couldn't help being here any more than I could.

The shepherd-looking Butch quit barking and thrust his grizzled muzzle against my free hand until I stopped and stroked him. Sheba, his black, long-furred companion, pranced stiff-legged. Her long fur was matted like dreadlocks or like a molting buffalo. She pawed at me, demanding I pet her, too.

Dogs are happy everywhere, I told myself. I could learn from them. I remembered my real dad telling me about the dogs he helped train when he was in the army. The dogs even learned to parachute beside their handlers. Flying dogs. Talk about alien landscapes. "They were happy as long as they were with their handler," Dad had said.

Plump brown hens and taller white chickens scratched industriously in the weedy grass patches as I walked around the corner of the barn. About ten horses lived here. Ten horses and one small burro.

From his metal pipe corral, Burrito lifted his pale head and brayed, long and sobby, as if he hadn't seen me in fifty years. Truth was I fed him a carrot before school this morning.

The bright chestnut Arabian stallion next to Burrito tossed his head, bugling a neigh, his long mane fluttering like torn flags. I slipped between the pipes into Burrito's corral. He was so little compared to the horses. His fuzzy crest with its raggedy mane barely reached a horse's chest.

Burrito was my only solid reminder of our recent San Gabriel Mountain past. The rest of my old world remained only in my mind now. We'd even sold the ancient furniture in our home. Francisco had dug up beds and dressers at garage sales for me and my brothers.

Occasionally, on clear days, the San Gabriel Mountains behind the Orange County hills sketched brown curves in the sky, fifty long miles away. An hour by car, a world away, a lifetime away.

We'd lived here now for exactly two weeks and four days. How was I going to keep my sanity?

I put my skateboard in the dusty tack room and took Burrito's red halter and lead line down from a nail in the wall. Tucking it under my arm, I picked up his plastic box of grooming tools and carried it to his stall. He stood, his back to me, munching something. I hadn't given him anything.

"What are you eating?" I asked and leaned down his long neck.

Orange foam dripped from his lips. A carrot. But I hadn't given it to him.

Sharply I looked up. A chainlink fence separated the six pipe corrals from the riverbed levee. Someone was scrambling up the steep levee hill. Someone about my age with hair as pale as Burrito's coat.

"Hey!" I shouted. "You leave my burro alone!"

The girl didn't look back, only accelerated up the hill and vanished over the levee.

2
A Flock
of Boys

Who did that girl think she was? You didn't feed someone else's burro. I'd have to build a wall at this end of Burrito's corral so no one would stick carrots into his pen. No one would have done that at home.

I led Burrito, still chewing orange spatters, to the tie rack and brushed his dusty hide until some of my anger fell away like bits of dander and old hair.

Next year about this time I could start riding Burrito a little. But he was old enough to pull a cart now. If I could find a cart. Maybe Miguel could help me build one. Something told me Francisco would help me build one, but words still stuck in my throat when I tried to talk to him.

Someday when Burrito could pull a cart, I would drive him back to the San Gabriel Mountains. I could take side roads. I nearly laughed to think of us on the freeway.

We'd just visit, though. No more running away. I'd tried that once, and it wasn't such a good experience.

Of course, for a burro in condition, fifty miles would only take one long day. We could do that, I decided. I could start training Burrito to pull something lightweight that wouldn't injure his growing bones and muscles.

"You'd like that, wouldn't you, Burrito?" I asked him. He looked at me from under half-closed eyelids.

A crow landed on the far end of the tie rack. Was it the same one who'd yelled at me?

"What do you want?" But it just flapped its wings and cawed piteously in a garbled, choked voice. "Oh, you're a baby," I said. "Where's your mom?"

As if in answer, another bigger crow landed beside the small one and proceeded to stuff something down the gaping beak. Then they flew off, the baby rolling sideways in the breeze. In the San Gabriels I used to see crows deviling sparrow hawks and being chased by mockingbirds. Did crows stay in the city? Weren't they migratory, or something?

When I had finished brushing Burrito and put the tools away, I reached for my skateboard, then stopped when my brain suddenly said, "Idiot! Burrito can start learning to pull you right now." Of course. I saw kids

17

on skateboards and roller skates all the time, their dogs pulling them along.

I'd kept some of the packing tack from our pack station for Burrito. I took a surcingle, a leather strap that buckles around the stomach like the girth of a saddle, and laid it over his back, lightly cinching it. Burrito just stared at me, unconcerned. Then I attached the breast collar, but I left off the crupper; it fit under the tail, and Burrito wouldn't like that too much. Besides, I didn't need it now. It was for steep mountain trails.

Burrito could pull me with the halter. The harness was just for him to get used to.

"Let's go, Burrito," I said, and we jogged away from the stables, an old white mare neighing jealously after us. We hurried along the dirt road, back onto my street, then down busy, four-lane Seventeenth Street up to the gate that finally led onto the levee. The girl I'd seen had climbed a couple of fences to reach Burrito, which was why we couldn't take her shortcut to the riverbed levee.

The Santa Ana riverbed was really only flood control, but it was the last bit of wildness for miles around. Would the riverbed keep me from going crazy in the city?

I studied the lines of the buildings. No, I didn't think the riverbed could do that.

At the edge of the riverbed, the landscape shifted. It ran north and south, a dirt trail on one side and a cement bike trail on the other side. Normally Burrito and I stayed on the dirt side, but it would be too hard for Burrito to pull me on my skateboard in the dirt.

In between the steep cement banks, the parched riverbed waited for the rare blast of water. In the meantime, somehow it busily grew tough weeds and bushes that sprang up from the silt carried downstream during fleeting rainy seasons.

Burrito and I crossed over a wooden pedestrian walkway. He paused, hung his head over the rail, and gave a conceited snuffle, as if to say, "I've been higher up than this," and he had. His little hooves clicked across the wooden boards.

On the other side of the bridge, I told him, "This is the beginning of your grown-up training."

He just yawned up into my face, his little baby teeth stained orange from that strange girl's carrot.

I balanced with my left hand, held the lead rope in my right hand, and firmly commanded, "Get up."

He knew that phrase and started off, his slim, neat legs flashing into a lively trot. The skateboard rattled next to him. He didn't even cock an ear; he was used to it.

Slowly I played out the lead line so that I dropped behind him. He needed to learn that I would be behind him, instead of beside him.

Since Burrito was used to us walking together, he slowed, peering at me over his furry shoulder.

"Get moving." I flicked the end of the lead rope into his ribs. He jumped sideways at the flick of the rope, yanking me off the skateboard.

"Whoa!"

He stopped, turned sideways, head up, both ears pointing at me in surprise.

19

"Okay, we'll take this slowly," I said and got back on my skateboard. I gripped the lead rope. "Get up."

He got up, and I played out the rope so I was just behind his left back leg. He kept his left ear back as if watching me through a periscope, but kept jogging.

Two bicyclists in jet black bike shorts and brilliant yellow and neon green shirts whizzed past on sleek bikes. They pointed at Burrito, and one shouted, "Trade you!"

Never in a thousand, billion years.

Burrito and I rattled down under the next bridge as streams of cars droned overhead. Some little kids about Andres' age on old Stingray bikes with banana seats rode toward us. One yelled obscene stuff about Burrito and me as they passed.

I pretended I was deaf and didn't respond. That's what they wanted: a reaction.

Weren't city people charming? I couldn't wait to tell Mom.

Burrito and I rolled past the back of my new school. The playing field brimmed bright green compared with the drab riverbed weeds.

In my two weeks at San Juan Middle school, where sixth grade was the lowest grade instead of the top like in my elementary school back home, I hadn't made any friends. No one even hopeful. Kids seemed to be off in little cliques and wannabe gangs.

I missed my best friend, Sean, like you miss walking firm on both feet. I limped through class.

Burrito jogged us past the school, so I pushed school thoughts into a mind closet and slammed the door.

Farther up along some rows of run down back-yards, I heard some furious barking, and two loose pitbulls, black with white bib chests, rushed out of some dusty evergreen bushes. Burrito slowed, laid back his long ears, and shook his head. The dogs halted and didn't come any closer. They kept barking but were afraid of my burro baby. Good thing because I was afraid of them. At another yard just before a bridge, four little kids behind a chain link fence called, "Burro!"

Burrito pulled me and my rattling skateboard under the bridge and back up again. Salt-and-pepper colored pigeons whirred out of the shadowed bridge into the sunlight. Cars and trucks roared by. Was the city ever quiet?

We passed a brownish green soccer field where kids my age in silky looking shorts and shirts kicked white and black balls, and ran and screamed, and jumped up and down. Andres was talking about join-ing a soccer league. Not me.

In the deep center of the riverbed, bushes grew like green troll hair. In the middle of one patch of dense brush a black plastic tarp stretched up into a lopsided tent.

Francisco said homeless people lived under bridges and in little camps all along the riverbed and to be careful. Most of them were harmless and didn't want trouble, he said, but a few were maybe burnt on drugs, and you had to watch out for them.

Shouts moved my gaze back to the trail. A flock of boys were ahead just off the bike trail. As I grew closer, I saw that one of the "boys" was actually a skinny girl with short black hair. She stood slightly apart from the group of boys who were moving in and out of the shadow of oak trees overhanging the bike trail throwing rocks into the shadows.

The boys' laughter and screams circled me and drew me closer. I could have turned back. I didn't want to get involved. But the girl's shrill voice caught my attention. Her fury matched mine.

Three boys bent to the ground, loading up with rocks. My stomach clenched. "Hurry, Burrito," I said and pushed the bike trail with my left leg, rolling faster and faster.

The girl stood watching in the sunlight. Then the boys with the rocks sprang inside the shadow of the tree.

I squinted into the shadows. Something small and dark hung from a tree branch.

3
The Hanging Tree

With a scream, the dark-skinned girl darted into the shadow and vanished. Burrito trotted faster. We were nearly there.

Two boys, one white, one Asian, suddenly hauled her back out. She kicked and maybe bit the white boy because he suddenly sprang away, cursing. Then coolly, the Asian boy kicked high, hitting the girl in the ribs. She dropped, curled over herself, her arms wrapped around her thin middle.

That was enough.

I leaped off my skateboard and bellowed, "Stop that!"

The girl didn't look up, but the kicker did, and his eyes narrowed more.

A couple of boys stepped closer. One still had rocks clenched in his fists. Burrito, with an angry grunt, his ears flat against his outstretched neck and his baby teeth bared, rushed at the nearest boy. He gave a burro squeal in the boy's surprised face. The boy fell back, eyes wide and scared.

I ran into the small crowd, shrieking, "Stop it! Stop it!" like a Harpy. For a mad moment I wished I was a Harpy, complete with long raking nails and poison canine teeth. I could be the avenger of helpless animals and skinny girls.

Well, at least I was one skinny girl they'd think twice about kicking. I shoved myself between two bigger boys, maybe eighth graders, and halted under the pitiful, hanging creature.

Burrito continued his assault, keeping the boys at bay.

The girl had gotten to her feet, and still holding her stomach, came up to me. "Can you get it down?" she asked, her words sharp and chopped off. "I cannot climb."

The creature was a small, gleaming black crow. He hung upside down, tight twine binding his legs, from a branch about six feet high. His wings frantically opened and closed, but he just swung in dizzy circles. He cried, not a grown-up caw, but a scared baby caw.

"Get out of—" began a white boy, but he didn't finish his sentence. Burrito lunged at him and then jerked back with a long rip.

The boy dropped his rocks, gripped closed his torn shirt, and ran. More boys ran after the first. Burrito savagely shook his head, the torn piece of shirt in his jaws. I dropped the lead rope as Burrito leaped after them, his little hooves flying. The strip of shirt flapped from his jaws like a tongue.

Boys scattered. Smarter ones dropped down the cement sides of the riverbed where burro hooves couldn't follow. The rest poured down the bike trail with Burrito in hot pursuit.

I turned back to the crow. He was still flapping his wings, but more feebly. Then he stopped and peered at me upside down as if to say, "What's taking you so long?"

Quickly I stood on my skateboard to scramble up a lower limb. From there I swung onto the branch the crow was tied to and scooted over to him. As I untied the twine, the crow curved his body up and tried to peck me.

"Cool it," I told him. "I'm helping you."

Just before the knot loosened, I gripped his scaly legs. The wicked looking beak slashed at my knuckles, but only thwacked like a dull stick.

"It is only a baby," said the dark haired girl. She still held her side with one arm. "The boys so cruel."

"Are you okay?" I called down to her as I balanced myself against the tree trunk with one hand, the crow in the other hand, feebly pecking my wrist.

"I could be worse." And she grinned white straight teeth at me. She was tougher than she looked.

25

Carefully, I held the crow against me. He wildly flapped his wings until I clamped them to his body. My whole hand just fit around him.

"He has spirit," said the girl as I carefully sat on the branch, held still a moment, then jumped. My ankles stung as I hit the ground.

Burrito trotted back, rope dragging like a lizard tail. He had dropped the material somewhere. His eyes rolled and his mouth was opened wide; he was laughing. All the boys were gone. Even the ones who had run down the cement sides had kept going.

"Good boy," I told him.

He sniffed at the crow. It pecked his nose and he jerked back with a snort.

The girl laughed. "Your donkey is funny, Reba."

"How do you know my name?"

She gave me a sideways look. "We're in the same class."

I almost squeaked, "We are?" but stopped myself. She didn't even look a little familiar. My sixth grade class was a mix of five white kids, two black kids, about twenty Hispanic kids, and fifteen Asian kids. Back at home, my real home, I had learned to say Asian, not Oriental. A friend used to say, "I'm not an Oriental, like a rug! I'm Asian."

As if reading my thoughts, the girl said, "*Bahn.* I'm Jantu and I sit two rows over from you. Who is that?" She pointed at Burrito, who was reaching up with his long neck and pulling down tree leaves to munch.

I remembered the pale girl who I'd caught feeding him carrots, and I didn't know if I should tell this girl his name, but that wasn't exactly fair.

"He's my baby donkey." I picked up his lead rope and slung my arm over his back to be sure she understood he was mine. "His name is Burrito."

Jantu grinned. "Good to eat."

"No!" I was horrified.

She laughed. "The burrito food, not him."

I wasn't so sure. Some friends back in the San Gabriels had brought home two guinea pigs once, and their Japanese grandmother had smacked her lips and asked, "How do you prepare them?"

Jantu looked into my face and started to laugh again, but then clutched her ribs, grimacing.

"Are you okay?" I asked again. Maybe the boy had broken one of her ribs.

She nodded. "I okay. Just inside sore."

I wondered if she would need help home. A steely part of me said, Forget it. You don't want to get involved, remember? She's part of this city.

The baby crow wriggled and jabbed at the soft places between my knuckles as if to prompt me.

"Do you live far from here?" I heard myself ask.

She pointed back to some apartments I'd passed. "There. I look out balcony and see boys and my cousin run by holding something. I thought puppy or kitten. So I follow. You know the rest."

Jantu held out her hands and gently took the baby crow from me. He pecked her fingers, but she spoke gently to him in another language and he settled down, blinking blue-gray eyes.

Jantu looked up and grinned, and I had to grin back. We began walking then. I tucked the skateboard under my arm, took the lead rope, and Burrito followed. Jantu held the baby crow perched on her wrist, his wings slightly lifted into the breeze.

"I'm surprised he doesn't fly away," I said.

"Too baby," she said and lifted a wing. "No flying feathers yet."

I wondered how she knew. "You said your cousin was with those boys?" I wondered if they were a baby gang or something. That would be something to tell Mama. You brought me to this gang infested city! That would get her. But if I said that, she might forbid me to walk along here. I wasn't willing to give that up.

"*Bahn*. Thay is my cousin, but he is a grade older. Ken and Jesse, they in our class."

I was embarrassed to ask which ones they were, so I asked, "Which one was your cousin?"

"The one who kick."

"Your cousin kicked you?"

She shrugged. "He's creep."

I would have chosen a stronger word.

We reached the metal gate of her apartments. She stroked Burrito with her free hand. "You take the crow."

"Me? I don't know much about birds."

"I not have pets in apartment," said Jantu. "And Thay live with me."

"Your cousin who kicked you lives with you?" I screeched.

"Hush, Reba." She put her hand over my mouth. Burrito's warm scent came from her palm. "No worry. Thay is nicer to me than he used to be."

She handed the crow to me. His talons dug into my wrist as he balanced. "Crows eat anything. But sure he gets, how do you say it, to make bones grow strong?"

"Calcium?"

She nodded, then unlocked the metal gate. As she slipped through, she said, "See you at school, Reba. Good-bye, Burrito."

"Bye."

Burrito and I walked back along the bike trail, the baby crow riding the currents on my wrist. Every once in a while he'd look over at me, catch my gaze and open his beak, begging for food, making awful gargling noises.

"When we get home, I'll feed you," I promised him. What, I didn't know.

Did the boys steal the crow from his nest? Why were people so cruel? I certainly wasn't like that!

Aren't you? a nagging voice asked. You aren't exactly pleasant to Mama or Francisco.

Oh, shut up, I savagely told myself.

4
Our
Own
People

When I got home from school, Mama wasn't home, but Francisco was. Weird.

"Where's Mama?" I asked.

"At the restaurant," he said and handed me a letter from Sean. I wanted to ask him if Mama was his slave or something. Why was she at work and he was at home?

Dear Reba,

School is out for the summer! Hurray! I went fishing with some other kids down at the gravel pits, but no one caught anything. Everyone except Darcy misses you. But you know how Darcy is. Are we gonna do something together this summer when you get off track?

Your friend,
Sean

P.S. The mountains aren't the same without you.

Darcy had this massive, slobbering crush on Sean. I just hoped he wouldn't fall for it, especially with me gone. And how could we do anything this summer when my new school lasted another long six weeks all the way into July? After that I'd be off track for six weeks, then back to school. All of Santa Ana's elementary schools and middle schools were year round. I'd never gone to school in the summer before. But even if I was off all summer, I wouldn't be able to see any of my old friends. The San Gabriel Mountains were just too far away. I wouldn't get a driver's license for another four years, and I knew Mama wouldn't let me take a bus so far.

I stuck Sean's letter in my English book. I felt worse after reading it. Life wasn't fair. Here I was, stuck in the city, going to school in the summer, and I'd probably get killed just walking to summer school.

Francisco had sat down on the couch, papers on the coffee table, a Diet Coke can next to his work.

"Bad news?" he asked.

"Yeah, for me," I said nastily.

His eyebrows went up, slowly, like he couldn't believe a kid could have real problems. "What's the matter?"

"Oh nothing major," I snapped. "I just read a letter from my best friend, who I'll probably never see again because I'll be killed by some stupid gangbanger."

"Wait, wait, just a minute." I had his attention now. Francisco sat up straighter, holding up his hand. "What are you saying?"

For a flash of a moment, I felt sorry for the tall, rumpled man, not far from a teddy bear kind of guy, but hey, he moved me here against my wishes, and now he wanted to know what was what. Well, I'd tell him.

I put my hand on my hip. "In case you haven't noticed, there is a lot of gang activity around here. I'm just a little worried, even though you're not, about getting, you know, assassinated." I paused and he just sat, staring at me as if a giant crane fly had dropped down and asked him to dance. "I guess Andres can wash the dishes in my place, so you won't have to worry about work not being done," I added as I stalked from the room.

For the next few days at school, Jantu would smile, say hi, and ask about the baby crow. Once she came over at lunch time and sat beside me—I was alone like always. But I couldn't talk much. I felt like I had peanut butter stuck in my mouth. After that she didn't try to sit with me at lunch. But she kept saying hi.

A couple weeks after the crow incident I walked home from school alone, thinking about how I would find out who was still giving Burrito carrots. Although I never saw anyone after that first time, I knew something was up because some days Burrito would have faint orange stains on his lips when I hadn't given him any carrots recently.

"Wait, Reba."

Shocked to hear my voice, I turned. Jantu was running behind me. She caught up, grinning.

"How is crow?" she asked.

"Getting bigger," I told her. "Still not flying though."

"He need someone to show him."

"Show him how to fly?"

"*Bahn*. Maybe you flap your arms and show him."

I laughed suddenly, imagining myself teaching him how to fly.

She grinned wider. "You do laugh and smile."

"Of course," I said a little crossly, but embarrassed.

She didn't say anything for a few minutes. We crossed the school field and entered the riverbed trail.

"You miss old home?" she asked suddenly.

How did she know? "Yeah, some," I said cautiously.

"Me too," she said.

I looked sideways at her, but she stared straight ahead. We walked under a bridge, from light, to shadow, back to light, and climbed back up to the levee.

"See mountains there." Jantu pointed to the faint stain of the eastern end of the San Gabriel Mountains.

Oh, I saw them, every day whether the sky was clear or smoggy, always achingly far away. Jantu wore a wistful expression, probably how I often looked.

"Khmer held many hills, mountains," Jantu said.

Despite my unspoken, practically unthought, vow of not getting involved, I was curious. "Khmer?"

"My home."

Was she Vietnamese or Chinese? Maybe from the Philippines. Was Khmer a big mountain or something?

"Where is Khmer?"

She pursed her lips and said, "Outsiders say Cambodia, but we say Khmer."

I couldn't even think exactly where Cambodia was. "When did you leave there?"

"I was only three-year-old," she said, the wistful gaze lingering and widening her dark, tilted eyes.

I swung my green backpack by the shoulder straps. "Do you remember much?"

"*Bahn.*"

I had figured out that meant yes in, what? Cambodian? Khmerian? Whatever her language was called.

"Hills are jungle, not desert like here. My uncle, aunt, my sister, and Thay, and me walk out of Khmer after the Vietnamese get rid of the Khmer Rouge."

"Who was Khmer Rouge?" I asked. I hoped that wasn't a Cambodian name for Americans.

She gave me a sad smile. "They our own people."

"You mean the Cambodians were fighting their own people?"

She nodded. I squinted at the disc of the afternoon sunlight. How much hate had it seen? I wondered. Her people weren't the only ones to turn on their own. My own Spanish blood recalled horrors.

"Look," said Jantu and pointed down into the riverbed. A house of black plastic rose above the bushes. "Lot of people with no home. My sister gives rice to some. My uncle gets mad, but she does when he at work."

"That's nice of your sister," I said. Much nicer than I was. "How old is your sister?"

"Sixteen. Her name Souca."

I wanted to ask more about her family, but something in her eyes, darker, blacker than mine, asked me to tell her something about my family. Be decent, Reba, I told myself. At least try to act like a Christian, even if you don't feel like one.

I took a deep breath. "I have three brothers. Pio, he's the oldest, is in college up in Pasadena. He didn't move down here with us. At home is Miguel, he's a freshman in high school, and my little brother, Andres, he's nine."

"So many boys," said Jantu. "Your mother is honored."

"Not hardly! They are pains!"

Jantu smiled at my tone. "In Khmer she would be honored."

"Isn't your mother proud of you?" I asked.

Jantu nodded slowly. "Because I'm safe, out of Khmer. *Bahn*, she be proud. But she is dead. My father, too."

"Oh." I swallowed hard. Stupid me. I should have figured that out. "I'm sorry, Jantu." It was the first time I'd said her name; the word tumbled off my tongue like a smooth, unusual stone.

Again she nodded, her short dark bangs bobbing over her eyes.

Life wasn't fair.

Who said it was?

Even God never said things would be fair.

But shouldn't life be fair?

"My family is all dead, but Souca and me," said Jantu, simply, like she was retelling an old tale. "Pol Pot, his army, kill my parents, my baby sister, and my older two brothers."

"But why?"

"Because my father a teacher and my mother journalist. They would have killed Souca and me, too, but we visited my uncle at the time of Pol Pot take over capital Phnom Penh where my family live. Intellectuals and families killed."

I recited suddenly, "Even wearing glasses was a capital offense, and you could be killed for they feared you could read."

Jantu gave me a startled look. "How you know?"

"School at home," I said, so into listening that I was talking sentences like her. "I mean, where I used to live. My teacher was into world history. But, Jantu, it seemed so unreal, not like anyone I knew was there."

Jantu reached over and squeezed my hand. "It past and I am alive. I live well. That best revenge. Now we see person in the tent."

She still had hold of my hand and began to pull me down the steep cement wall. What if the person in the tent was a creepy drug addict?

She let go of my hand to balance herself. I stopped.

"Do you know this person?" I asked.

"Think so," said Jantu. She gestured to me to keep coming, but I planted my feet.

36

"Have you met him?"

"Her. I see from balcony."

"That's right. You and your eagle eyes." She grinned widely, so I followed her.

In the riverbed I sank to my ankles in deep sand. At each step my feet broke through the fine crust on top, crunching, but underneath the sand was dense. Sort of like Burrito's coat. His outer fur was stiff, but his under fur was deep and soft.

In the middle of the riverbed, a thin, dark trickle of water cut through the sand. Growing up along the water were thick bushes of castor and young shoots of spindly bamboo.

Jantu hopped over the water. Francisco's words paraded in my head: "Don't mess around at the campsites of the homeless. Some of them are nice, but some are loco." I hoped this wasn't one of the loco ones. But if Jantu knew her, wouldn't it be all right?

Jantu pushed through a bunch of branches. Pollen puffed up and I sneezed after her.

The tent, really just four sticks stuck in the ground with plastic trash bags stretched over them, sat in a small clearing. "Kayla, you here?" Jantu called.

Silence. A pure white egret rose up from a clump of tall grass, its long yellow legs dragging behind. Then its wings gained height from the earth, and the bird floated into the light, lovely and free.

Cars whooshed over the Seventeenth Street bridge. A siren wailed. A helicopter thumped over us.

"I guess she not here," I said, nervous.

But behind me a soft voice said, "I'm here."

5
The Riverbed Home

I thought it was you, Kayla," said Jantu triumphantly, tossing her short black hair.

A girl about our age walked slowly toward us on the footpath, pushing aside scratchy branches. Her pale hair shone in the sun. She was from our class, I could see now, but she was taller than everyone else. She never raised her hand to answer questions, but if the teacher called on her, she always knew the answer.

"Spying on me, Jantu?" Kayla tipped her head like the baby crow when he would study me.

Jantu laughed. "I spy on everyone in this riverbed."

Kayla began to smile, but then I hollered, "You're the one feeding my burro!"

Kayla's smile faded into a wary look. "So."

"So! You just don't go around feeding someone else's animal," I said, but Kayla just shrugged.

Jantu stared at Kayla, then at me, then back at Kayla. I crossed my arms over my chest.

"Leave my burro alone," I demanded.

Kayla's face flashed with anger. "Fine," she said through gritted teeth. "It's a stupid burro anyway."

"He isn't!"

She tossed her head. "He is."

"Shut up!" commanded Jantu. "How we be friends if you fight?"

"Friends!" Kayla and I both said at the same time in the same shocked tone.

"Friends," said Jantu firmly. "Now, Kayla, show us inside tent."

"Do I have a choice?" asked Kayla.

I wanted to just stalk away, but I was curious about this girl who lived in a tent and fed my burro carrots on the sly.

Kayla pushed back the flaps, ducked in, and led us into her tent.

The air was still inside even though the plastic sides and top rippled like water in the sideways lake. The trash bags had been opened up, the sides carefully cut, neatly sewn with heavy thread. I peered closer.

"Dental floss," Kayla said.

The bottom edge of the tent was tied to an undergirding of long branches with more dental floss.

Inside the tent the light was grayish as if we were sideways and underwater. A sideways lake. That fit my crazy change of life. The bottom of the tent house was smooth white sand. I could tell Kayla had raked it and raked it until the sand was free of rocks, leaves, and twigs.

"Sit down." Kayla waved us to a crooked, thick chunk of branch. We perched. She poured water from a plastic milk jug into an assortment of chipped mugs. She handed Jantu a blue and white one, me a green one, and herself a purple and white striped one.

Jantu wrinkled her nose. "This not Santa Ana River water, is?"

"Just yours," said Kayla, smiling, as she sipped her water.

I started to drink when water poured down my chin and onto my shirt. "Hey!" I jumped up, dropping the cup.

Kayla put her hand over her mouth, trying not to laugh. I snatched up the cup, examined it more closely, and saw a fine crack from the rim down about an inch.

"You gave me this on purpose," I said.

"Yup," said Kayla, satisfied.

Jantu sputtered into her water. I could leave and never talk to either of them again. I hesitated, then set the cracked cup on the sand.

"Can I have a different cup?" I asked Kayla.

"Can I feed your donkey carrots?"

We stared each other down, like two strange dogs.

"Okay," I said reluctantly. "Carrots are good for him. Apples, too. But nothing else. Not even grass. It could have pesticides on it."

"I know that," said Kayla indignantly, and she poured more water for me into an unbroken cup.

We sat quietly for a few minutes, drinking. Outside, shouts and yells floated down from the bike trail.

"So I guess this is like your hideaway place?" I said.

"It *was*," said Kayla, giving Jantu a pretend glare. Jantu just chuckled.

"See, I live in the same apartments that Jantu does." Kayla twirled a lock of her pale hair. "It's so crowded at my place. I have to share my room with my younger sister and brother. So this is like my own room here. Sometimes I even come at night and bring a little candle." She said the last part defiantly.

"You be careful," said Jantu. "You know this is F-Troop area. And my cousin tell me about new Asian gang."

Kayla shrugged and set down her mug. "They don't even notice me. Besides I'm going to cover the tent with more branches to camouflage it. You guys wouldn't want to help, would you?"

We scouted outside the tent for long, slender branches heavy with leaves. At the edge of the narrow water, I reached for a good branch, but the sand ledge crumbled and my feet plunged into the water.

I wrestled with the branch trying to break it from the bush. Kayla came over with a small knife and sawed at the branch until the tough fibers parted. Then together we dragged the heavy branch back, dug a hole, and hoisted it upright so it hung over the tent.

"I need a bunch more to hide it," said Kayla.

"But they'll dry up and look fake," I said.

Kayla shook her pale hair. "Look at these bushes. Most of them are pretty awful looking and they're still growing. No one will notice a bunch more branches, dried or fresh."

I wondered why she wanted to hide. But then didn't most people hide from something or someone?

We gathered about ten more branches and arranged them around the tent. A blister formed on my palm, then popped. Jantu's arms were scratched, and a red welt burned across Kayla's cheek.

The tent was better camouflaged. The sun had lowered, burning deep orange and red shadows, and the heat had faded like a turned off oven.

"I look out my window in the morning," Jantu said, "and see if branches are new and improved."

A flock of crows flapped overhead, soaring low along the riverbed. An idea popped into my head. "Kayla, would you like to have a mascot at your tent?"

She gave me a suspicious look. "What do you mean?"

Jantu jumped up and down. "I know what you're to say, Reba."

"What are you talking about?" demanded Kayla. "What mascot?"

"A crow baby," I said. "Jantu and I rescued this baby crow and he's really interesting, but he's messy. Mama isn't too happy about him walking around in my room pooping everywhere. I can't keep him outside because I'm afraid a cat will get him, and I don't have a cage."

Kayla's blue eyes softened. "You mean keep him in the tent?"

"*Bahn*," said Jantu. "He's safe in here."

"We can take turns feeding him each morning," I said. "And then after school we can come here and feed him and—" I broke off.

And we'd be invading her hidden space. Maybe Kayla didn't want us here all the time. After all, she'd made the tent to get away from people.

"Is that okay?" I asked Kayla. "If you don't want us around, just say so. Or if you just want the crow—"

She pursed her thin lips and twirled a lock of pale hair. "You're both okay," she said finally. "Bring your crow baby tomorrow."

"Oh, well, thank you for telling we okay," said Jantu, "Your Majesty." Jantu bowed formally.

Kayla gave her a friendly shove. "Get out of here. I want to be alone for a few minutes before I have to go back to the maddening crowd."

"I'll bring the crow baby tomorrow morning before school," I called.

"I'll be here," said Kayla.

I wondered if she stayed overnight.

"In the morning I check for tent and bushes and tell you," Jantu said and waved to me, then turned to hike back up to the apartments.

I waded through the skinny river, my shoes still wet anyhow, and headed the opposite way home.

Mama would be glad to see the crow baby leave because he was so messy. If I'd had a cage I could have kept him at the stable with Burrito. But now he shared my room, and he dumped wherever he happened to be. He refused to stay on a perch for long. Every morning I laid down newspapers all over my floor and bed, but he still managed to squirt places I hadn't covered.

Mama said he sat on my bedroom windowsill while I was at school and pooped down the wall. I was forever wiping up his messes.

I thought about sneaking out to the riverbed late that night to see if Kayla was still in her tent. But if Mama caught me I'd be in major trouble. Besides, was it my business what Kayla did?

6
The
Last
Laugh

After I got back from the riverbed, Mama and I made dinner in the kitchen. We had new dishes from Francisco's mother who lived in Mexico. She came up for Mama and Francisco's wedding on a Trailways bus with two heavy wooden boxes tied with hemp rope, full of green and blue earthenware. I took five dishes down from the cupboard, placed them around the table, and began laying silverware beside each plate.

When Mama and Francisco opened wedding presents, Miguel had asked, "Did you pay custom tax on this?" Fortunately Francisco's mama, my step-grandmother, didn't know much English and Mama, with a dagger glare, dragged him away before any explosions happened.

Actually, she was pretty nice. During the wedding I sat next to her, and she held my hand, whispering every few minutes, "*Bueno*." I guess she meant she was glad he was marrying Mama.

Later she gave us kids presents, too. Not junky stuff like you'd get some kid you didn't know, but thoughtful things. For Andres, a red, yellow, and blue handmade kite sewn from shiny material. For Miguel—not that he deserved it—a cool leather vest. For me, a long, full, red, green, and white cotton skirt. The colors of Mexico. When I twirled, the skirt stood out around my knees, heavy and rich. I loved it, which is saying a lot because I usually hate dresses and skirts.

While Mama and I got dinner ready, Francisco, Miguel, and Andres sprawled on the couch in the living room watching some dumb baseball game. Was that fair? Not that I wanted to watch a bunch of men in funny outfits chase a ball.

"Tell them dinner's ready," said Mama.

I poked my head out the door. "Hey, you bums, dinner's ready."

"Reba." Mama sighed.

Miguel crossed his eyes at me, but Francisco smiled and turned off the television. Andres didn't move. He was in a trance, or something.

"Hey, kid." Miguel poked Andres' foot. Andres still didn't move. "He's asleep," Miguel exclaimed.

"Poor kid." Francisco stroked Andres' forehead. "He's warm."

"Just leave him," I said. "I can save a plate of food for him. He's coming down with a cold or something." The kids down the street had been snotty-nosed ever since we'd moved here three months ago.

Francisco lumbered to the kitchen with Miguel trailing after him, and they plopped down at the table. We passed around enchiladas with lots of cheese and the green salad that I made. I wanted to plant a garden, but the backyard was nearly as bad as the front. Dirt and weeds. I imagined my garden, lush with tomatoes, chile peppers, green peppers, and big, fat carrots for Burrito.

"Reba," said Mama.

Miguel was laughing through a mouthful of beans.

I turned my head slowly and blinked away the images of myself picking baskets of vegetables, herbs, and bright flowers.

"Did you hear anything I said?" Mama's eyes probed me.

"My name."

Miguel yelped with laughter. "I told you," he chortled. "It's got to be a guy."

As if I wanted a guy. The only male in my life was Burrito, and that's all I wanted.

"I was thinking about planting a garden," I said sternly.

"She's in the ozones."

"There's only one ozone, Miguel."

He just hooted and made kissing noises. "She's thinking about a boy."

"Shut up."

Miguel started up after me.

"Stop, now," said Mama in a hard voice. "Both of you."

Miguel slowly sank back into his chair and mouthed, I'll-get-you.

"I'm so scared." I yawned and stuck my tongue out at him.

"Reba," said Mama sharply, and I shut up.

"It's good we decided," said Mama to Francisco. "God knows, they need it."

Both Miguel and I stiffened.

"Need what?" Miguel asked and looked over at me. Miguel and I were suddenly united.

"Going to church," said Francisco as if he were saying going to the movies or to the store. "We found a church nearby with a good youth department."

Suddenly I was angry. Did Francisco tell Mama what I'd told him about the gangbangers and getting killed? As if going to church would keep me safe.

"Church!" Miguel exploded. "I'm not going to church!"

"Me, neither," I said through clenched teeth.

"Oh, yes, you are," said Mama. "It'll be a good way for both of you to meet some nice kids."

"Around here?" I asked doubtfully.

"Nice kids are boring," said Miguel.

Mama silenced us with a look.

I always had the no-church excuse of living up in the mountains with no one to take me except my Aunt Kate, and she didn't get up that far very often.

"I'm not going to any church." Miguel glared around the table. "You can't make me either."

Mama snorted. "Oh, yes, I can."

"How?" he challenged.

Without a word, she shoved back her chair, sprang up like an emboldened coyote, and marched to the kitchen sink. She snatched up a huge butcher knife and stalked back to Miguel.

"You will go to church." She loomed over him, the light from the overhead bulb glinting off the blade.

Miguel screamed like a woman. "Not again, Mama! I'm still healing from the last knife wounds."

Francisco started laughing as Miguel ducked under the kitchen table, his rear end sticking up. Mama smacked him with the broad side of the knife. Miguel roared and crawled under farther. I was laughing too hard to kick him.

"Church," said Mama, brandishing the knife, "begins at nine-thirty."

"Nine-thirty!" exclaimed Miguel from under the table. "Sunday is my only day to sleep in."

"Not anymore," said Mama.

"What's going on?" Andres stood in the kitchen doorway rubbing his eyes. "Why is Miguel screaming?"

"I'm disciplining your brother," Mama told Andres, then turned to Miguel. "Consider yourself warned."

She carefully laid down the knife and got a plate for Andres. He just blinked at her, not awake.

Miguel crept out from under the table, sat down, and stuffed a forkful of enchilada in his mouth. I caught his eye.

"What about you and Mama?" I asked Francisco, innocently.

"What about us?" he asked.

Miguel caught on immediately. "Yeah," he said. "What about you and Mama?"

"What do you mean?" repeated Francisco.

"You're going to church with us, right?"

Francisco and Mama exchanged guilty looks, and I knew I had them.

"You have to set the example," I said triumphantly.

Miguel was grinning, madly. "That's right," he said. "I'll go to church only if you go, too."

"We're going to church?" asked Andres in an amazed voice.

"The church has a good youth department," said Mama, a little desperately.

"And these youth, they have no parents?" I asked. "Are you sending us to a church of orphans?"

"Very funny, *m'ija*." Mama cut her enchilada with the side of her fork as if she wished it were my words.

"Well?" demanded Miguel. "All of us or none of us."

Mama and Francisco looked knowingly at each other, and Francisco said firmly, "We'll all go."

Miguel and I grinned at each other. How long would Mama and church last? She didn't even like going to weddings or christenings, and the things she said about TV and radio preachers and priests were unrepeatable.

Then Mama, Francisco, Miguel, and I looked at each other and cracked up. *Maybe we are a family*, I thought.

"Hey, what's so funny?" asked Andres, still half asleep.

"We're all going to church!" I yelled.

Andres just said, "I'm hungry," and sat down.

So am I, I thought suddenly.

7
Tea
Egg
Morning

The next morning about six-thirty when I took the crow baby into the pearl dawn, he blinked his smoky-blue eyes like Andres had last night. He swayed on my arm as I eased the front door shut and stepped carefully down the three wooden stairs. Mama and Francisco's bedroom was in the front of the house, and their window was cracked open.

Not that I was doing anything wrong, I told myself. Mama would be thrilled that the crow was gone. But she wouldn't be too thrilled that I was in the riverbed.

I detoured by Burrito's stable. He was down, his neck curved like a bowstring, his nose brushing his hind hooves. He was a pale puddle in the unpeeling dawn. His long ears flickered. He flared his nostrils, catching my scent, the one he'd known from birth, maybe even before he was born if what some scientists say is true.

He sat up, yawning, then stood on long, coltish legs. Chickens, brownish red, black and white striped, and big whites, were waking up, clucking, scratching the dust in the hazy morning. The marine layer, Francisco said it was called. Ocean fog. I drew a deep breath, hoping for salt. But the air only smelled like moist dirt, even though the ocean was just ten miles away.

The crow baby, fully awake now, opened his beak and gave a giant squawk.

"Okay, okay," I said and set him on the top pipe of the corral. Burrito pointed his ears at me and squawked a funny bray. Was he imitating the crow baby?

"You funny thing." I kissed his soft nose. "I'm totally efficient this morning," I announced as a red and black tailed rooster strutted by, eyeballing us. I fished in my backpack for crow baby food in a plastic baggie: wet bread mixed with high protein and high calcium baby cereal.

At the store Mama had groaned, "I can't believe I'm buying baby food again. And for a crow."

The crow was glossy black, healthy looking, so the food must be agreeing with him. If only he'd fly so he could go back to being wild. He gave another insistent caw, then begged, head tipped back, beak gaping wide, his wings bent and flapping helplessly.

I stuffed the sticky bread mess past his mouth, into his throat. He gurgled and gargled like an underwater monster, until he swallowed the goop into his crop, the weird place where birds begin to digest their food. I'd read about it a couple of days ago from a book I'd checked out from the Santa Ana main library. If nothing else, all that goop made a lot of poop.

Burrito ambled over, dust fluttering under his gray belly, to see what he was missing. I shoved another lump down the crow's throat. He shut up for a minute, his crop bulging.

"Now for you," I told Burrito and took two carrots out of the backpack. Burrito smiled, his upper lip curled up, and neatly took one carrot, crunched it messily, drooling orange foam, then delicately lipped the second carrot from my fingers. More orange foam boiled around the corners of his mouth.

Suddenly the crow baby spat out a wad of bread. The rooster snatched it and ran off, two black and white hens pursuing him.

"Gross!" I exclaimed.

Burrito only tossed his head and drank from his automatic water bowl, then lifted his face, more orange foam and water mixing, dripping to the ground.

I could only laugh. "At least you animals don't care about what others think of you. I bet it makes your lives easier," I said, coaxing the crow back onto my wrist. I wished I didn't care what others thought.

"See you after school," I said to Burrito.

He gave a small snuffle as if to say, "Oh sure, go off and leave me. See if I care." When I looked back, he was hanging his head through the pipe of his corral watching me with sad eyes. I wished I could take him with me.

Maybe I would ask the teacher if I could bring him to show the younger kids, sort of a show and tell. These city kids never got to see animals like burros except on television. Burrito was gentle and would never kick or bite unless they were mean like Jantu's cousin and his nasty little friends.

At the riverbed I jumped the trickle, the crow flapping his wings to keep his balance on my arm. We reached Kayla's tent after winding through some yucky sticker bushes. Kayla poked her head out of the tent and grinned.

"Make enough noise," she said. "I heard you coming forever."

"I didn't know I was supposed to sneak up," I retorted.

The crow baby squawked. A couple crows overhead cawed in return, then circled, studying us and the crow child. Crows are into extended families, I read in the library book. And they are very smart, recognizing human faces if they've seen them even just once. They will mob or attack a hated human, dog, cat, hawk, or anything else that threatens them. I eyed the crows overhead in case they decided to dive bomb us.

Kayla just said, "Look what I found."

She opened the flap and I crawled in, crow and all. In the corner was a sturdy, upright collection of branches, like antlers, planted firmly in the sand. A perfect perch.

"Hey, crow baby, your new home."

I lifted him up, and he stepped off my wrist onto a twisted, horizontal branch. He began to preen himself, ducking his head against his stubby tail and poking through the baby feathers on his wings. He seemed to hardly notice the carefully arranged branches as if to say, "Of course, I deserve the best."

"I looked and looked for those branches," said Kayla. "I finally found them down in the golf course."

"When did you have time to get them?"

It was barely seven now, and when I'd left last night it was nearly dark.

She shrugged. "Before you came this morning."

"You must get up early," I told her and waited.

She gave me a wary look, almost like the look the wolverine gave me back in the mountains when I first saw him up in a pine tree near our house. A look that said, "I'm not sure I can trust you."

Kayla just said casually, "I like to get up early."

"So do I," said Jantu, coming into the tent, a bag in her hand. "Best time of the day. When wonderful can happen."

Jantu stroked the crow baby's head as I dipped out some more mushy food. He saw me and opened his beak with a hoarse cry. I stuffed a wad of mush down his throat, and he gargled like a sore throat medicine commercial. Jantu and Kayla giggled.

"He sounds like my uncle sleeping," said Jantu.

I grabbed a mug and asked Kayla, "Do you have any more water?"

She lifted a plastic bottle up out of a hole in the sand. "Keeps it cooler," she explained and carefully poured the water into the mug.

I showed it to the baby, then set it down in the sand, away from the branches so he wouldn't poop in it.

"What's he called?" asked Jantu.

"I haven't been able to think of a name," I said. "What's crow in your language?"

Jantu frowned. "I don't know. I forget a lot. My uncle makes us talk English at home. He says to forget Khmer."

"You shouldn't forget," said Kayla savagely. "If you don't remember, who will?"

Jantu seemed struck dumb by Kayla's ferocious tone.

Kayla turned to me. "What is crow in Spanish?"

I tried to recall. "*Cuervo* is like a raven," I said, slowly. "And *corneja* is a kind of crow, but I don't think this kind." I bit my lip trying to remember. Names of things were the hardest to remember, words I didn't hear much anymore.

Kayla made an exasperated sound. "You two are cultural rejects."

I stuck my tongue out at her. "And what about you?" I asked. "What is your culture?"

She shrugged. "I'm a mutt."

"No, you are purebred American," said Jantu. "That is best of all."

"Not hardly," said Kayla. "I think my family was from Ireland. And I don't know Gaelic, so I guess I'm no better than you guys. Anyway, we're going to be late to school."

I looked at my watch. "Nine minutes," I said.

As we left the tent, Kayla carefully opened the front flap and dragged a rusted part of what looked like a bed springs and propped it in front of the tent.

"So our baby doesn't escape, but gets air," she explained.

"I forget." Jantu suddenly climbed over the headboard, then came back with a paper sack. "Breakfast."

As we hurried up out of the riverbed and along the bike trail, a shortcut to the back of the school, she handed around peeled, hardboiled eggs, but brownish, not like any hardboiled egg I'd ever seen.

"Are these, like, rotten?" Kayla wrinkled her nose.

"*Bahn*, I'm give my friends rotten food. Dummy. They tea eggs. Don't you know anything?"

Friends, I thought dazedly. Was that even possible in the city?

Kayla made a face, but bit in. "Good," she admitted.

"*Jas*, good," agreed Jantu, taking a big bite.

I guess I didn't know anything either, so I bit into the egg and to my surprise it tasted smoked. Like a smoked cheese or meat. "If it's rotten, then rotten eggs are good," I said, and we gobbled down all six tea eggs, two each.

"Last one to school is a rotten egg," announced Kayla, and she began to run.

I flew like the crows, with Jantu on my left, Kayla on my right. We even got to class on time. A small miracle. Mornings were a wonderful part of the day.

8

Siege!

After school I ran home and got Burrito. Mama and Francisco were usually at one of Francisco's restaurants until five or six. Who knew where Miguel went, and Andres had quickly made friends with the neighbor kids across the street. The neighbors had offered to watch Andres in exchange for free dinners at Francisco's restaurant, so everyone was happy, I guess.

Everyone but me. Poor little Reba. Get out the violins.

I skateboarded down the street, while Burrito walked briskly beside me. He still didn't approve of walking in front of me.

Was it true? Was I unhappy, or was complaining about my miserable life simply a habit? I probed my feelings like one would touch a newly healed, fractured bone. Is it healed? Or is it still sore? Did I really want to go back home to the mountains?

Yes, I was miserable here. If I had a choice I definitely would go back. But I didn't have that choice.

When I stuck my head in the tent, the baby crow squawked madly.

"I try feeding him," said Jantu, "but he spit the food back out."

I tied Burrito to a nearby bush and left him to nibble weeds. Kayla rushed up to croon over him and pulled out a carrot like a magician with a rabbit.

I glanced at the crow baby and his food. If I'd learned nothing else in this city, I'd become an expert in feeding baby crows.

"The food's too dry," I explained and added water to the cereal until it was a sticky mess. Then I shoved a glob of it down his throat.

"Ick," Jantu commented.

"I know, but it's what he likes." I globbed another wet ball down his throat and another and another until he sat quietly, blinking his eyes, digesting or whatever birds did in their crop.

"He needs name," Jantu said as she wiped up the bird splats from the sand with leaves and tossed them into the bushes.

"How about Pooper?" I suggested.

Jantu rolled her eyes. One thing I had noticed about people learning English; they usually got the slang down pretty fast.

SIEGE!

"How about Ebony?" Kayla called as she lavished Burrito with strokes over his shoulder, his neck, his fuzzy mane. He was steadily ignoring her to munch leaves.

I wrinkled my nose. "Ebony is sort of overused."

Undaunted Kayla said, "How about Onyx?"

"What is that?" asked Jantu.

"It's a rock," Kayla answered. "A black rock. It's glossy, sort of like glass."

"What are you? A geologist?" I asked.

Jantu repeated, "Onyx. I like."

It fit. Ahh-nix. I liked the way the word snapped to the end. I said to the crow baby, dried food on his beak, "We christen you, Onyx of the Black Wing." Solemnly, I touched his ruffled head and each wing arch with my index finger. Onyx lifted a talon and scratched his head vigorously. "Animals are so . . . so . . ." I searched for a word.

"Unselfconscious," supplied Kayla.

"That's it. They don't care what you think. They just do what they have to do."

"I know," said Kayla. "That's why I like animals better than people."

Before I could comment, a shrill war whoop arrowed into the tent.

Outside bushes rustled. Burrito brayed. Onyx yelled and fell off his perch. Fear leaped through my veins.

We ran out of the tent.

We were under siege.

Four boys, one white, two Latin, and one Asian, leaped out of the bushes in front of the tent. Jantu

61

clutched my arm. Two of the boys held machine gun squirt guns, the other two held sharpened sticks. They were some of the same boys who had thrown rocks at Onyx.

Kayla snatched up two rocks the size of golf balls and tossed them from hand to hand, real casual like. I had to admire her. The girl had style.

"What do you guys want?" Kayla demanded.

"We want our crow back," said the white kid. He was in my class, and his name was Ken.

"It's not your crow," I snapped.

"You hurt it," said Jantu. "You cruel."

"That's right," said Thay. "And you'll be next."

Four against three wasn't fair.

But we were smarter. My eyes narrowed. We'd show them.

"If we give you the crow, will you go away?" I tried to sound scared.

Kayla and Jantu gave me stormy glares: traitor!

"Sure. All we want is our crow back," said Ken, all confident.

Thay smiled and stepped closer. His teeth were even and small. I ached to pop him with my fist right in his mouth.

"To start, I guess you can see him if you want," I said, still trying to sound cowed. "Ken first, okay? The crow gets nervous with strangers."

Grinning, Ken swaggered up to the tent opening. Kayla started forward, but Jantu caught her arm, a gleam in her dark eye.

"Put down your arms first," I said, blocking the entrance.

"Huh?"

"Your squirt gun, stupid," said Kayla.

He gave her a dirty look, but handed his machine gun to the Hispanic kid, Jesse.

I stepped aside. Ken went in. As I ducked under the tent flap after him, I gave Kayla the most intense look I could muster. A flash crackled between us, and she relaxed. The flap crinkled behind us.

"Where is it?" asked Ken. He was taller than me and had to bend over.

"He's not an it!" No way did they care about Onyx.

"Okay, where is he?"

Onyx was cowering as if he knew he was in peril.

"You guys scared him. He's under here." I reached under the branch tangle and touched the stiff feathers.

Outside a boy yelled. Sand pelted the side of the tent. More yelling—boy or girl? I wasn't sure.

"What's going on?" demanded Ken.

I gave him a helpless girl look and lifted my shoulders.

He jumped up. He started out, but I neatly stuck out my foot, and he fell full length, face in the sand.

I launched onto his back. He yelled. Furious. He tried to throw me off. He rolled. He plunged. But I clung to him as if he were Uncle Hector's Medicine Hat horse that time she bucked me off. She had succeeded. He wouldn't.

More yelling. One of the boys shouted, "Ken! Ken!" I threw my weight forward onto his shoulders so he couldn't sit up. He wriggled and hopped like a pinned worm. I kept shifting forward as he tried to kick me with his heels. After getting me once, he only whacked himself in the butt.

Despite my weight, he managed to gain his hands and knees and crawl out of the tent, me still astride his back. Kayla and Burrito, now untied, were rushing after Thay and Jesse. They all plunged into the bushes. The boys yelped each time Kayla hit one with a rock.

Jantu was screaming something. It was eerie and shrill, deep and growling, too, sort of like you hear on *Kung Fu* or maybe like on *Star Trek, The New Generation* when Worf spouts off in Klingon. Thay screamed back at her. The other boy, Pepe, darted in the opposite direction, getting the heck out.

When Thay and Jesse had run off, Kayla and Burrito returned. Jantu stood grinning at me. I was still on Ken's back. He would periodically jump up, fall back down, try to roll over and pin me, but I'd thump him hard with my heels and he'd right himself.

"Looks like you got a tiger by the tail," said Kayla. Or a Ken by the backbone.

9

Crow
Captors

"Okay," I said, thinking like mad. "Here's the plan." What I needed was something really big to keep Ken from bothering us and Onyx again. Gee, Reba, that's called blackmail.

Ken spat sand and tried to kick me in the butt again.

"Better behave," Kayla warned as she put her foot on the back of his neck.

He groaned, turning his head to the left, and laying his cheek on the sand. He closed his eyes like he was giving up, but his muscles were too tense under me.

I leaned over his shoulder and spoke clearly into his ear, "We will let you go only under the condition you get up and immediately leave and do not come back."

"And if I don't?"

"The burro here kicks the daylights out of you." Kayla led Burrito closer. A vine trailed out of his mouth. His fierceness was hard to see.

"He is trained," I said, carefully. For what I guessed I didn't have to say.

"Trained to do what?" asked Ken. "Look stupid?"

"To attack," Jantu said.

"Oh, how dumb can you get?" Ken squirmed.

"I guess you better tell us since you're the dumbest one here," I said, sitting tight.

"Sheepherders use donkeys as guard animals," announced Kayla in ringing tones. She increased the foot pressure on his neck until he coughed and quit moving. "They fiercely guard sheep from dogs, coyotes, even wolves. This little donkey is capable of killing you in one kick."

What a professor! I stifled my laughter in a coughing fit.

"Okay, okay," said Ken. "I believe you. Now let me up."

"When I let you up, you better start moving fast out of here," I warned him.

"And never come back," Kayla reminded him.

"Okay, okay," he repeated.

Since I didn't want to sit on his back for the rest of my life, I leaped off him. Jantu tossed me a stick. I caught it and held the smooth branch tight before me.

Ken climbed to his feet. Sand peppered his jeans and T-shirt as if he'd been part of the wall of a fallen sand castle. He warily glanced around.

"Get out of here," roared Kayla. "Now!" She punctuated her words with a rock. It stung his arm.

"Okay, okay." He trotted along the narrow path, shooting looks back over his shoulder. Kayla threw another rock that hit his heels, and he leaped into a run.

"Never come back," shouted Jantu, shaking a squirt gun over her head.

He ran up the cement side and vanished down the bike trail. The three of us looked at each other and cracked up laughing. I bent over, I was laughing so hard. Burrito merely ran his gaze over our heaving bodies as he chewed on a vine.

I wiped my eyes. "We got their guns. Cool." I picked up a mega machine squirt gun.

"I'm bad," I said and aimed it at Kayla.

"Mercy, mercy," cried Kayla and put her hands over her face. That set us off laughing again.

The baby crow walked out of the tent, striding along the sand, making fine footprints. He squawked loudly.

"Hello to you, too," said Jantu. "Want gun?"

The thought of Onyx defending himself with a squirt gun in his talons set me off again.

"You know those boys will be back, don't you?" said Kayla.

"I know." My plan hadn't been so earth shattering after all. A very temporary stall for now.

Jantu sighed. "Ah, my cousin. Such pain."

"Will your cousin get you later?" I asked.

She shrugged. "It doesn't matter."

"Yes, it does," snapped Kayla. "They can't go around terrorizing us. We should have beaten Ken up to show Thay what we'd do to him if he hurts you again."

I shook my head, thoughtfully. "Then everyone tries to hurt each other more and more. When does it end?"

Jantu said fiercely, "When we kick butts."

"If only we could turn them to our side," I said.

"You mean like friend!" Jantu was shocked. Her dark eyes blazed. "They are worse than animal. They hurt Onyx."

"No offense intended, Burrito," said Kayla to the grazing donkey. "Animals are better than most people."

"Those boys," said Jantu. "I don't even know the words in English."

"They are little wannabes," said Kayla. "All they understand is a kick in the head."

"Wannabes?" I asked.

"You know, they want to grow up to be gang-bangers."

We were quiet for a few minutes. This I could tell Mama. A real accusation. See, these kids who are almost gang members tried to beat me up—

Mama would ask, "What were you doing? Where were you?"

The riverbed.

She'd forbid me to come here again.

Things got so complicated. I sat down in the sand, and Onyx climbed onto my leg and perched.

"So now what?" I asked.

"We gotta defend ourselves," said Kayla.

"How?" asked Jantu.

I was thinking that I didn't want to be part of the we. I mean, who wants to invite trouble? I didn't have to come here anymore. Kayla and Jantu could take care of Onyx. Pretty soon he'd fly away anyhow.

"We dig deep pit around the tent," began Jantu.

"And what? Fill it with snakes?" Kayla shook her head. "Maybe," she said, "we could get permission to bring Onyx to school for an assembly or something and when they see how important he is they'll at least leave him alone. Like, peer pressure in the opposite direction. If they bother us and Onyx, we tell kids at school and everyone gets after them."

If it would work out that way. "We have those oral reports about California history," I said. "That might help."

"What do you mean?" asked Kayla.

"We could choose the Gabrielino tribe for our history report. Crows were in Gabrielinos' religion and mythology." I almost said, "In my people's religion," but I was afraid Jantu and Kayla might make fun of me or worse, not believe me. "One thing the Gabrielinos thought was that crows advised when strangers approached." I paused a moment, then added, "He almost did, didn't he?"

"I think he was more the cause of the strangers' attack," said Kayla. "But I get what you mean."

"How you know about that? Are you Gabrielino Indian?" Jantu asked.

"Part Gabrielino," I said, my cheeks flushing. I wasn't sure why I was embarrassed because I believed I really was, even though it was all an ongoing debate in our family. My oldest brother, Pio, was an anthropology major in college, and he didn't think so. "My real father has said we are of the Gabrielino tribe," I told them. "Most of those Indians were killed in the late 1800s by white men."

"Don't people ever stop?" asked Kayla bitterly.

The three of us locked gazes for a long moment, and a deep sorrow pierced me.

Finally Kayla broke the spell. "I can feed Onyx tomorrow morning."

"Thanks." Mama wouldn't like me zipping out early every single morning. I knew I'd better get home now or I'd be in trouble.

I grabbed my skateboard and tugged on Burrito's halter. "Come on, you lazy beast." I sounded like Mama when she used to prod the pack burros on the trail. "Get moving."

Once out of the riverbed, Burrito pulled me easily up the cement path. Dark orange stripes rippled the western sky, and through the top of the line of eucalyptus trees, a star shimmered. The first star tonight. What did I wish for?

So many things that they didn't fit into one wish.

Burrito paused to snatch up a mouthful of grass. On the street I let a bunch of little kids pet him. They'd never seen a live burro before.

The first star still shone over my shoulder as I opened our front door.

10
Star
Music

Ken and his mangy friends didn't bother us at school the next day, which was Thursday, or on Friday either. Saturday morning as we gathered at Kayla's camp, Jantu told us that the night before she'd found an unsigned sheet of lined paper with a skull and crossbones slid under her bedroom door. Duh, like, who was it from?

"Cousin Stupid," said Jantu.

As we fed Onyx outside under cloudy skies, the four boys zipped above us on their bikes and made obscene gestures.

Kayla observed, "They're licking their wounds."

Jantu burst out laughing. "Like dogs!" she chortled. "You are so clever."

Kayla gave her a bored look. "Where did you grow up, girl? Thailand?"

"Shut up!" Jantu shrieked and flung herself at Kayla, who dodged. They ran through the bushes, and I finished feeding the hungry crow baby as their whoops and screams bounced off the cement walls.

When they came back panting and giggling, I said, "Hey, I've got an idea."

"Stop the presses," said Kayla.

I ignored her. "Let's move our camp and really hide it so the boys can't find Onyx again." Or us either for that matter.

"Our camp?" asked Kayla.

I hadn't even realized I'd said that.

"I cannot spy on Kayla if we move tent," complained Jantu.

"I'm sure you'll find a way," said Kayla dryly.

So the rest of Saturday we looked for a new nesting site as Kayla called it. Finally, on the other side of the overpass we found another thickly bushed place. It was a little closer to my house, but not much farther from Kayla and Jantu's apartments. It wasn't quite out of sight of Jantu's balcony, but she'd have to look really hard to see much.

We carefully took down the plastic sheets, then lashed together the branches that were the tent poles, and laid the bundles over Burrito's skinny back. He didn't mind being a true pack burro, and he minced along the sandy path to Onyx's new home.

Kayla's new home, too? I wished I dared to ask her. I wasn't sure why I didn't. Maybe I was afraid of her answer.

The sky deepened from pink to scarlet as Burrito pulled me home on my skateboard. My arms and shoulders ached from lifting and carrying Kayla's stuff and setting it all back up, making sure it was well protected by a new cover of branches.

At the stable the first star slid into folds of smoky orange clouds.

"Starlight, starbright," I began, then stopped, like a burro halted with a curb bit.

A wish wasn't stronger than a prayer, was it? Stars couldn't have more power than God. He made the stars. They were just a bit of glitter in his hand. My Aunt Kate, who teaches at CalTech, once said God calls each star by a name. And in the Bible it says the stars sing together. Aunt Kate also told me that some radio astronomers claim the radio static stars emit sounds like music. Some stars have bass voices, some alto, and some soprano. Their music is to the glory of God.

So I gave my prayer to a star to be composed and sung to God. I thought he'd like that.

Sunday we went to the church Mama and Francisco had picked out. All of us. Mama and Francisco, too. Miguel kept grinning sideways at me.

"We'll see how long this lasts," he whispered as we tumbled out of the car.

Andres went to little kids' church, Miguel to the high school Sunday school, and Mama and Francisco into big church, as I heard some kids call it. I went to the junior high Sunday school up on the second floor of the building next to big church.

My heart lurched as I walked into the huge room. About forty kids were talking and laughing, some sitting on metal folding chairs set in rows, the rest standing in various half circles.

The mountains felt more like God's house than these buildings, but I guessed God could live anywhere. When the Israelites were crossing the desert with Moses, God lived in a tent, kind of like Kayla's.

I gingerly sat on an aisle seat in the back so I could make a fast getaway if I couldn't take it anymore. I could always hide in the bathroom. A couple seats over sat a cluster of girls who looked like seventh or eighth graders. They definitely wouldn't pay attention to me, a lowly sixth grader. They wore high heels and nylons. I studied my black tennis shoes; not a brand name, just tennis shoes.

I wondered if I had made a mistake in wearing my same old jeans. At least I was wearing the new neon green and pink sweater Mama had gotten for me last month, and I'd French braided my hair. I was good at braiding; I used to practice on some of our burros who had longer manes. I pretended they were show horses getting ready for a show.

What if these kids thought I was fresh from Mexico? Without a green card, even. No one would want to sit by me. My face burned a little. Maybe no one would talk to me because they'd think I didn't know English. But then I thought, *Heck, I don't want to talk to any of them anyway.*

I was just about ready to get up and hide in the bathroom for the next hour when a man the color of asphalt said into the microphone, "Take your seats. We're about ready to start."

They all sat down. If I got up now and left, everyone would see me. So I stayed.

I could hardly drag my gaze from my tennis shoes to look up front where an older girl with long curly red hair was plugging a guitar into an amp. Behind her an Asian guy with straight inky hair almost as long as hers plunked himself down in front of a set of drums.

At least this church had people of color. What if everybody here were white? Then how would I feel?

I looked around. I saw Hispanic, white, Asian, and black, boys and girls, and most had on shorts or jeans and casual shirts. I relaxed a little.

The first song started, and of course, I didn't know it. Two girls, one white and one Hispanic, entered my aisle, crossed in front of me, then sat next to me. They looked close to my age. The Hispanic girl wore a skirt, but no nylons, just jelly sandals. The other girl had on jeans and a bright orange shirt. She sat beside me, flashed a smile, and began singing the words I didn't know.

I liked the music, especially the red-haired girl's guitar riffs, but since I didn't know the songs, I sat woodenly. The group sang five songs. At least I could clap along with everyone and not sit there like a colicky burro.

When the music faded, and as the musicians untangled themselves from their equipment, the white girl beside me held out a pack of bubble gum.

"Want some?" she asked in a friendly way.

"Sure, thanks." I took a stick gratefully.

She leaned over to her friend and offered her a stick, too, then took one herself. "Are you new?" she asked.

I nodded, chewing.

"Do you go to San Juan Middle School?"

I nodded again.

"I thought I'd seen you there," she said, which surprised me. "Who do you have?" she asked.

I told her my teacher's name, and she gave me a mournful look.

"Lucky you. She's brutal. At least the term is almost over, and you'll get a new teacher. I had her last year. I'm in seventh grade, and so is Ida, but we're almost in eighth. At least when they let Ida out of rehab."

Ida snapped her gum and slugged her friend's arm. "Don't tell her stuff like that. She might believe you."

I laughed with them, and then the black man, I guess he was the leader, began to pray.

"I'm Deb," whispered the girl with the gum.

"I'm Reba," I whispered back, then closed my eyes and tried to concentrate. It was hard because my thoughts bounced around like a rock falling into a ravine.

Still, I could hear the music of the stars in the distance.

11
A Change in the Weather

Monday after school, Kayla, Jantu, Onyx, and I sat down inside the tent, the flaps open. Burrito munched weeds outside the tent door. Clouds flickered overhead, bunching up, then running like a herd of wild horses, all white and gray with manes and tails and legs.

"Look at Onyx," said Jantu suddenly.

The baby crow was perched on his branch, staring silently up and out of the tent at a flock of crows wheeling and diving in the wind. He flapped his wings, not like his hungry flutter, but with firm strokes as if he wanted to join them.

"Go on, Onyx," encouraged Kayla. "You can do it."

He strained his neck, arched his back, and pumped his wings. He stepped up and down as if on invisible stairs. His feathers ruffled in the breeze that waffed the plastic tent sides.

Suddenly, bushes crackled, and the tent plastic snapped. Burrito tossed his head startled. Onyx squawked his baby cry and fell off his perch. Then someone yelled, "Get her!" and Jantu, Kayla, and I jumped up.

Pepe darted into the tent, roughly picked me up under the armpits, and began to drag me out. Jesse appeared and yanked me off my feet while Pepe held my arms. Kayla and Jantu rushed at him. Too late. They dragged me out of the tent, breaking truce.

Burrito brayed angrily. Someone shrieked. A rock flew over me and thunked solidly. Burrito squealed in pain. My burro! I screamed and lashed out with my whole body, but the boys didn't let go. Kayla rushed near me.

"Help Burrito!" I screamed at her.

She hesitated, then flashed past us, Onyx tight against her chest. Jesse and Pepe lugged me in the opposite direction, Jesse in the lead, holding my legs like one would hold the poles of a stretcher. I kept trying to kick him in the butt, but he was stronger than he looked and managed to keep my legs stretched out so I couldn't gain any momentum.

As they carried me farther from Kayla's camp, a third boy appeared. Ken. They kept chugging me along the narrow path.

I'd have to break away on my own. I couldn't rely on Jantu and Kayla. They were dealing with Thay and another kid. So to save my strength and to lure them into carelessness, I went limp as if all the fight had gone out of me.

They carried me under the ancient railroad trestle. Pepe and Ken had traded places, so Ken now held my arms. He and Jesse carried me sideways, both facing me.

I closed my eyes halfway, trying to be really limp. Maybe they'd think I'd passed out and put me down.

Drops of water fell on my face, and my eyes flew open. For a moment I thought it was raining. My muscles tensed. The Santa Ana riverbed was like the dry washes in the San Gabriel Mountains: flash floods. But almost as fast as another drop hit me, I realized Ken was sweating on me.

If I protested, he'd just make sure all of his sweat plopped on my face. So I said urgently, "Guys, I'm getting motion sick. I'm gonna barf unless you let me walk."

Jesse hesitated and Ken said, "She's lying. No one gets motion sick being carried."

"What do you know about it?" I asked. "Why do you think I don't ride my burro? Riding him makes me barf." I hoped they didn't realize Burrito was too young to ride.

Ken sighed. He stopped and told Jesse, "Put her feet down."

Jesse rudely dropped my feet. I gave a sudden, wild leap, but Ken still gripped me hard. He bumped the backs of my knees with his knees, and I went down on a prickly bush.

"Ow!"

Ken yanked my arms behind my back and pressed me onto my side. I struggled and got sand in my mouth.

"Take off your belt, Jesse," Ken ordered.

I watched Jesse suspiciously as he pulled off his narrow black belt. Were they going to whip me? I tensed, preparing for a huge effort to resist.

But Ken merely said, "Tie her hands behind her back."

Jesse knelt down, his knees crunching on the sand, and looped my wrists together, tight. My shoulders ached, and I bet bruises bloomed on my upper arms.

Ken leaned his weight over me to keep me flat in the sand. "Jesse, take off my belt for me," he said.

Material and leather slid together in a fast rush. "Loop it above her knee," Ken instructed.

Jesse did and with a quick movement, Ken let go of me, and was on his feet with the end of the belt in his hand.

"Get up," he commanded.

"Who me?" I asked.

"Very funny," he said. "Get up."

"No," I said. I knew what would happen. I'd get up and he'd jerk me off my feet. Forget it. I had enough bruises, thank you very much.

Ken swore long and loud. He used a few words I'd only heard once or twice before.

"I'm impressed at your fluency," I told him.

He glared at me.

"You want me to kick her?" offered Jesse.

"I didn't hurt you, Ken," I said. "This isn't fair." That fairness thing again.

"I'm teaching you a lesson," he said darkly.

His teaching I didn't want.

Then his eyes lit up. I dreaded seeing that light. I knew I'd wasted a star wish, a star song, hoping we could be friends. Stupid. How naive could I get?

"Don't kick her," Ken said. "Start digging a hole, Jesse, a hole big enough to put her in."

Terror ran through me.

I tried to catch Ken off guard by bolting, but he had a death grip on the belt around my knee. He jerked me off my feet, just like I'd predicted. I ate sand again.

Jesse dug a hole like a shallow grave. Surely they wouldn't bury me completely, would they? My teeth began to chatter and the wind was no longer a friendly crow lift, but chilling. Behind us, the clouds grew darker, blocking most of the sun.

Ken held my arms and Jesse grabbed my legs and they swung me into the hole. Ken held me down while Jesse started scooping sand onto my legs, stomach, arms. I'd be trapped if they anchored me with much more sand. Night was coming and who knew when Kayla or Jantu would find me, if ever. I could see the newsflash: Girl's Skeleton Found in Riverbed.

So I kicked. I struggled. Sand flew. Once I latched onto Ken's forearm and bit him, hard. Warm metallic taste tanged my tongue. As Ken hollered, a dark cloud fell on him, silencing him.

12

Circle of Crows

Ken ran away, bent over, his arms covering his face. A dozen crows, more or less, wings the breadth of umbrellas, dive bombed him, chasing after him. The crows boiled over me, too. I couldn't protect my face since my arms were tied, but the crows never touched me. Only their fierce beating wings doused me with bits of sand and a lot of wind.

The crows also chased after Jesse, who had leaped across me in my shallow grave, yelling and shrieking as he ran. The crows appeared as a black cape, billowing after him.

For a moment I lay dazed, blinking, my eyes tearing from the sand swept up by so many flapping wings. My heavy blanket of sand trapped me, and my chest heaved as I tried to gain my breath.

The two boys ran fast with arrows of crows after them. This was definitely the weirdest thing that had ever happened to me.

Around me a couple of crows lingered in the taller bushes, their feathery chests puffed out, their wicked beaks open. Torrents of caws flooded out as if they were trying to explain something to me, louder each time, like I was a stupid child.

Then I realized: I'm free. No wonder the crows thought I was stupid. I kicked at the sand, then crawled out of the grave on my elbows and knees. Once out, I wriggled my hands until the belt loop slipped, and then I unbuckled Ken's belt from my knee.

I stood on shaky legs. Sand splintered off my clothes in glints of sparkling gold. The two crows in the bush opened their wings and soared away. Up higher, they joined the circling flock of crows, all screaming, like a kettle of bouncing black beans.

I was free. The crows had freed me.

I picked the belts back up—evidence—and I broke into a jog, heading back to Kayla's camp. Burrito, the girls, Onyx. What had happened to them?

Deep sand slowed me, but I plowed through as fast as I could, my leg muscles aching. And as I ran, strength poured back into me. Free, I was free! I ran through the shadows of the train trestle and looked up to see a couple of little kids balancing overhead on the ties. They shouted down at me, "Hey! Those birds helped you!"

"They did!" I called back. Wildness and vibrant freedom burst through me. "Wasn't it great?" I added.

They were silent, so I told them the only explanation I knew: "God sent the crows to help me."

They stared at me big-eyed, then broke into shouts like songs. I ran on.

When I came to Kayla's tent, everyone was gone. Burrito's little hoof prints were everywhere, and in between his hoof prints were tennis shoe prints. A large bunch of both kinds of prints led toward the golf course. I followed them, my heart pounding.

Overhead the circle of crows had spread out in the red-streaked afternoon sky. More groups of crows joined them, flying in from distant trees and rooftops. They wind-tumbled north up the riverbed. Passing them on their way south were bunches of gulls, heading for the ocean. Where did crows go at night? I wondered.

My name floated on the wind. I froze. Then I realized it was a girl's voice, and I relaxed. Up on the levee trail near the back of Jantu's apartments, the two girls and Burrito stood, the girls calling and waving. Burrito joined in, heeing and hawing.

I climbed out of the riverbed as fast as I could, slipping once on the smooth cement wall, and scraping my knee. When I reached them, Burrito rushed to me and thrust his nose under my arm. I stroked his softness between his ears.

"Thay and Pepe hit him with sticks," said Jantu indignantly. "Right on his shoulder."

I knelt and studied the welt. Once Mama had agreed to buy two pack burros, sight unseen. They came in a rickety old trailer, the floor mucky with urine drenched straw. Both burros had whiplashes over their shoulders and flanks, even on their legs. The wounds had healed after several weeks, but if anyone picked up a stick, even months later, they panicked completely. Burro flashbacks, I guessed.

"Poor Burrito," I said softly and stroked his nose. I hoped he wouldn't shy from sticks now. "I've never hit him." I straightened up and saw that Jantu had a black eye. "Jantu! Your eye!"

She shrugged. "I'll live."

"Her wonderful cousin did that to her." Kayla's eyes flashed. "We'll get him back. But worst of all they got Onyx!"

"What!" What would they do to him? "What can we do?" I asked.

"Get him back," said Kayla grimly.

"Declare war," said Jantu, her eyes blacker than any night I'd seen.

Somehow I was sure Onyx would be at Ken's house. "Does anyone know where Ken lives?"

They both shook their heads.

"We follow Ken home after school," said Jantu. "We steal crow back."

"It's not stealing," said Kayla. She asked me what they did to me and I told them, uncertain how to explain the crows. But Kayla and Jantu didn't seem too surprised.

Kayla punched the sky in triumph. "Onyx's relatives are helping us!" she said.

"So, how did you two guys get away?" I asked.

Jantu and Kayla exchanged grins. "I hid in bushes," Jantu said. "Kayla ran and they chased her."

"Then I ran in a big circle." Kayla took over the story. "When I passed by the bushes Jantu was hiding in, she ambushed them."

"I threw sand in their faces," said Jantu.

"I can tell you, that slowed them down," said Kayla. "Then I grabbed Burrito and we took off out of the riverbed. They didn't follow us."

Too busy running with Onyx, I thought.

"I thought Kayla had Onyx," said Jantu.

Kayla sighed. "And I thought Jantu had him."

The sun was nearly gone. We agreed to sneak after Ken tomorrow, and reluctantly I said goodbye.

Kayla and Jantu walked together to the apartments while Burrito and I walked to the wooden bridge and crossed it back to my part of the city.

The city. Where boys beat up girls and torment innocent animals.

Late that night I woke up, tears running down my cheeks. I turned over, bedsprings muttering. A slice of my dream curved around me. The boys had someone in the grave they had dug for me. In a weird, dream way the boys weren't Ken or Jesse, but some unknown boys. And it wasn't me in the grave, but Kayla; they were burying her. My legs were buried in sand so I could only stand there and cry out, "But she's too young to be buried." All around me people in black feathers were laughing their heads off.

It took me a long time to fall back to sleep.

13

Some
Spies

The next day at lunch we sat on the grass under a eucalyptus tree by the big dumpster just on the edge of the school grounds. Since I'd started school here, already two big trashcan fires had roared out of this dumpster.

When we finished making plans about how we'd follow Ken after school, Kayla said darkly, "Ken better be taking good care of Onyx. I have this friend who's a pastor. Maybe I could tell him about the boys stealing Onyx. He knows Ken."

"What could a grown-up do?" I asked. "Make Ken give us the crow back, but that doesn't mean the boys will leave us alone." The whole thing made me weary. My thoughts circled around and around like a bit of broken leaf in the wind. If we hadn't moved to the stupid city all this wouldn't be happening.

"A pastor?" asked Jantu.

"Church," I said. "You know, that place where you worship God?"

Jantu crossed her eyes, and Kayla laughed suddenly. The wind rippled her pale hair into one wave. "You know, Jantu. They must have churches or temples in Khmer. Where lots of hypocrites go."

"Hypocrites?" Jantu looked at me for an explanation.

"People who tell you to be good, then aren't good themselves," I said.

"Like my cousin," said Jantu wisely. "Is the church your mother makes you go to that way?"

Now I was the church expert. What a laugh. "Hypocrites are all over the place," I said, wanting to be fair. "But shouldn't church be a place to learn how to not be a hypocrite?"

Kayla grinned. "They got you brain-washed already, Reba."

"They have not!" I glared at her. "It's not God's fault that people are hypocrites."

Jantu looked over our heads. "I see a couple hippo-critters."

Ken and Jesse walked across the scraggly grass. Jesse's neat, small figure and his dark, straight, slicked back hair gave him a smooth, urbane look. Ken was stockier, wider, and moved like a confident alley cat, free and lively, his wide blue eyes fixed unwavering on Kayla, then me. What nerve.

I had their belts at home as proof of what had happened. I'd stuffed them between my mattress and boxspring and prayed that Mama wouldn't do any serious cleaning for a while.

As the boys got closer, I stood. I didn't want them looming over me. Kayla unfolded her long legs; she was a lanky egret of a girl. She tossed her pale silky wing of hair over her shoulder. Then Jantu rose, crossed her arms over her chest, and glared defiantly out of her good eye.

"Where's our crow?" I demanded, hands on my hips. The closest lunch monitor was a short Hispanic man wearing a Mighty Ducks hockey cap. He was posed at the seam between the blacktop and the grass, too far away for my liking.

"First, tell us how you got those crows to help you yesterday," Jesse blurted.

Ken's arm went out and Jesse rocked back. "Cool it," Ken hissed, and Jesse snapped his jaw shut.

"Hey, Reba," Ken said, and I realized it was the first time he had said my name. I didn't like the way he made it sound. Reee-baa. Like a sick sheep.

"Yeah, Ken," I bit his name off. "You crow snatcher."

"We had him first," snapped Ken.

"You hurt him!" Jantu shouted.

"Where is he right now?" asked Kayla.

Ken snorted. "Like I'd tell you."

"We'll find him," Kayla said confidently and tossed her head. She and Ken stared one another down for a long minute. A small, unclear thought wriggled into my brain. Something about Kayla and Ken—

The lunch bell rang.

Ken broke the stare and said, "Later." He wheeled around. Jesse stayed right beside him, his voice trickling back to us: "I want to know how she called those crows down."

So do I, I thought.

Kayla pulled back her arm when a man's voice said, "I wouldn't do that if I were you. Not unless you want detention."

"Busted," whispered Jantu.

Kayla slowly lowered her arm. A half-eaten apple was in her hand. The teacher-monitor waited, smiling. Kayla dropped the apple into the trash can, and he walked on.

"Life is unfair," said Kayla through clenched teeth.

Tell me about it, I wanted to say, but instead we went to our lockers.

When the last bell of the day rang, Kayla, Jantu, and I shot out the door and scattered in three directions. I took up my post near the water fountain, taking nervous drinks every so often.

Kids streamed past me. Some stopped for water, glanced at me, then went on. The bike racks were across the blacktop. Kayla peeked out from behind the handball backstop. Jantu was supposed to be out by the front gates.

Finally Ken, Jesse, Pepe, and Thay walked together down the outdoor hall. I turned my back, pretending to drink from the fountain. They walked inches past me. I hardly dared to breathe. Was this

90

how private investigators felt? Ick. I didn't like the way my heart hammered in fear.

The boys sauntered away together, Ken and Pepe pushing their bikes. As they turned the corner of the school I scurried after them, peering out from the corner of the building.

Someone touched my shoulder.

I jumped and started to yelp when Kayla clapped her hand over my mouth. "Gosh, you'd make a lousy spy," she said.

"Good," I muttered. "I don't want to be a spy."

"Come on," she ordered, and we slunk down the street a half block behind the four boys. At the corner Thay and Jesse went toward the apartments, but Ken and Pepe swung onto their bikes.

"Oh great," I groaned, breaking into a run.

Jantu was across the street, her long hair beginning to fly as she kept pace.

I was panting hard, but Kayla was falling behind, even though she had longer legs. All my mountain climbing was paying off, I guess. Too bad it was wasted here in the stupid city.

Jesse waved and wheeled down a street while Ken kept riding straight ahead. How far away did he live? He never once looked back. Good thing. The more tired we got the more we straggled and didn't keep hidden. Some spies we were.

But Ken never did look back. He pedaled down the street, then made a turn into a new housing tract, where all the houses looked the same. He turned the corner.

I rounded it a moment later, but he was gone.

14

Out of Control World

"Okay, check yards for his bike," I said.

"Or a name on the mailbox or something," said Kayla.

"What's his last name?" I asked.

Kayla made a face. "Morse. We always end up near each other because my last name is Moore. We've gone to the same schools since first grade." She scrunched up her face even worse and added, "I've been sitting next to him for six years! Yuck!"

We hunted in front yards and peered over fences into backyards, until Jantu waved wildly. She pointed at a small front porch with a wooden sign hanging from a cross beam. It read: Morse Family.

"Bingo," said Kayla. The front yard was empty of bikes and crows. "Climb on my back," Kayla said to me, bending over at the back fence gate.

Gingerly I put a foot on her narrow back, grabbed the top of the wooden fence and swung up, trying to keep most of my weight on the fence.

The backyard was bigger than ours with lots of trimmed grass, a couple of flowering trees, and Ken's bike lying on the patio. Best of all was a wire cage with a crow in it!

"Onyx!" I said excitedly, and did a little dance.

"Ouch!" hollered Kayla. "Not on my backbone."

"Sorry." I jumped onto the sidewalk and she stood, rubbing her back.

"Now what?" I asked.

"Kick the door in?" said Jantu hopefully.

"Girl, you belong on the SWAT team," said Kayla.

"Let's just do what's simple," I said.

"What's that?" asked Kayla.

"Walk in there, take Onyx, and walk out again."

"Okay," said Jantu. "Is gate locked?"

We pulled the wire latch, and it swung open.

"Easy," I said.

"I hope so," said Kayla.

We cautiously slipped into the yard. I shut the gate but didn't latch it for a quick getaway. We kept as many trees and bushes between us and the back of the house as we could. Who knew? Maybe Ken was sitting and looking out the window.

Onyx appeared to be dozing on a perch inside the big cage. The cage was sitting against the wall of the house under an open double window. Red and black striped curtains fluttered lightly, and I guessed that might be Ken's bedroom. I just hoped Onyx didn't make too much noise when he saw us.

A hedge grew alongside the patio, and we crawled beside it. Fortunately, Onyx's cage didn't have a lock on it. I wished the cage wasn't so big, or I'd have taken it too. It was a nice cage.

"You get him," said Kayla. "We'll wait here for you, okay? Less noise with one."

I swallowed hard and tried not to be chicken. I'd make a lousy thief. My heart was pounding harder than it did when we were chasing Ken on his bike.

On all fours I crawled onto the cement porch and scurried like a crab to the cage.

Ken's voice rolled out of the window. "But I don't want to go with you that weekend. Dad and I are planning to go to Anaheim Stadium for that car show."

I jumped from fear and nearly fell over.

A woman's voice answered, "What has your father been saying about me? Is he bringing up that bit about the hospital again?"

"No, Mom. We have plans. That's all."

A chill ran through me. When I was younger I wanted to be invisible so I could walk through people's houses and listen in on their conversations and see what they did when they were alone. Being here was like that, only it wasn't fun. It was creepy and gave me a sick feeling in my stomach.

"I have a court order that says I can see you two weekends a month," the woman's voice rose in tempo. "Your father can't do this to me."

"Mom," protested Ken. "It's not like that."

I had to get us out of there. Swiftly, I unlatched the cage. Onyx blinked back his eyelids and stared at me, stunned looking. Before he could squawk, I grabbed him to my chest and ran back to the hedge.

"Let's go," I whispered. We didn't even try to hide. We just pelted out of there.

Behind us Ken's and his mother's voices twined together in an unpleasant twist, arguing hotly, accusations flying like fiery darts.

They didn't even see or hear us rush out of the backyard and shut the gate behind us. I didn't want to pass his house again, so I ran the opposite way down the street, and we headed back to the riverbed by a different route.

Several blocks from Ken's we slowed, panting, and I released Onyx from my death grip. He yelped in protest and climbed onto my shoulder, preening his mussed up feathers.

"At least he looks okay," said Kayla.

"Yeah," I said and stroked the baby crow. I didn't feel bad about taking back our crow, but I felt sick about what we'd overheard. The words burned across my brain, like a brand. For the first time I felt sorry for Ken as a kid caught in something he had no control over.

I knew how he felt.

15

Consider
the Ravens

The next day after school, I expected Ken to roar up and demand the crow back, but he didn't. After picking up Onyx from my house, Kayla and I then hurried to the stables to get Burrito.

"I just love him," Kayla confessed, burying her face in his stubby mane.

"You two are almost the same color," I said. Burrito in his pale coat and Kayla with her fair hair.

She smiled and I realized how little she really and truly did smile. Usually, she just cracked sarcastic jokes. But when she smiled, her whole face lit up as if little Christmas lights were flicked on inside of her.

"I daydream that I have a horse who loves me and follows me around like Burrito follows you around," she confessed.

"What kind of horse?" I asked as we went through the gate off the street and into the riverbed.

Kayla led Burrito by his peppermint pink and green lead rope. "An Arabian stallion," she said immediately. "Chestnut colored, all bright and shiny. I'd train him to be like those war horses, to rear and jump on command."

I smiled, thinking of Uncle Hector's Medicine Hat Horse. She reared and jumped, but not on any command. We were lucky if she just stopped on command.

A couple of pickup trucks painted orange rumbled along the opposite levee on the cement bike trail.

"What are trucks doing there?" I asked.

Kayla shrugged. "Early this morning they were cleaning the storm drains in the riverbed."

The weather forecast was predicting rain here and in my old friends, the San Gabriel Mountains. I'd had Onyx with me since last night, and this morning, I'd fed him. So why was Kayla down at the riverbed early in the morning?

I wasn't sure how to ask her, so I just plunged in like you're supposed to do in cold water. "Do you sleep overnight in the tent?"

Kayla, her right hand on Burrito's narrow withers, where his neck ridge met his back, froze. But then she said dryly, "What did you think? That I slept *on* my tent?"

She was so prickly!

We walked a few minutes, then she said, "Onyx is so funny at night. He wakes up if I light a candle or turn on a flashlight, and he talks to me in this low voice, like a whole new language, rough sounding. Sometimes he just goes on and on. I wish I knew what he was telling me." She leaned close to the bird sitting on my shoulder. "What are you saying?" He cocked his head, and the sun dimmed behind a bank of clouds piled high like a bowl of mashed potatoes.

"You're changing the subject," I told her.

"I know." She stared across the riverbed. "Okay, I usually sleep in my tent most nights."

"But why?" I couldn't understand how her parents didn't know. Or maybe they did?

"Because I hate my room, okay?" she snapped.

"That's a stupid reason," I said.

"No, it isn't!" she shouted straight into my face.

I stopped, shocked. Burrito stopped at the same time. That invisible umbilical-like cord that has tied us to each other since his birth was still strong. The lead line jerked, and he forced Kayla to a halt.

Her eyes, her whole face was furious, and she glared fiercely at me, as if I were responsible. Maybe in a sense I was because I kept asking questions when most people were poked to a stop by her thorny answers.

My heart was hammering like that time Sean and I were lost in the cave, and we were trying to get out. But this time it was Kayla who was lost, and she didn't want to find her way out.

"Do your parents know you sleep there?" I asked softly.

"My stepdad does," she said stiffly and put her arms around Burrito's neck. He curved his head over her back and looked up at me with questioning eyes. "My mom works at night," she said, her voice muffled in his fuzzy mane. "I only sleep on the riverbed when she's at work."

I wondered about that. "Doesn't your step-father—" I began. But she pulled back from Burrito and said, "Jantu will wonder where we are."

That time I knew better than to press her. Maybe later I could ask her more.

At the edge of the golf course, we scrambled down the soft dirt and scraggy grass into the riverbed. A few crows swirled overhead, cawing. Onyx and I listened to them. Last night I had looked up *crow* in my Bible, but the only crow listed was when the rooster crowed three times when Peter denied the Lord.

So then I looked up *birds* and under that listing was sparrow, then raven, which isn't a crow, but a close relative to the crow. First, I read the verse in Luke: "Consider the ravens, for they neither sow nor reap . . . yet God feeds them; how much more valuable you are than the birds!"

How funny—"consider the ravens." God wanted us to think about birds. A few black crows ruffled the sky, and I wondered if they were told to consider the people? I glanced at Kayla. Her face was as stormy as the clouds gathering in the north, against the mountains. Someday I'd tell her that verse, that God thought she was valuable.

I'd found another verse in Genesis about how Noah let a raven go from the ark to see if the waters from the flood exposed any land. Funny, you always hear about the dove Noah let out of the ark, but a raven went first.

Last, I had read about Elijah, a prophet guy God had told to hide. So Elijah did and then some ravens brought him bread and meat, morning and evening. Where did they get the food? Maybe a woman was baking some loaves, set them on the table to cool, when along comes a raven through the window—did they have screens on their windows back then? The raven picks up a loaf of her bread and flies off with it. I smiled, thinking of a woman like Mama, yelling, chasing the bird with a broom, but each time it gets away with the bread.

Did the raven have to find different houses each time? Or maybe God told some woman in a dream to bake bread twice a day and set it out and a raven would come and carry it away. Wouldn't that be weird? The neighbors would think she was crazy, like people thought Noah building his ark was loco.

Then I wondered if the meat the ravens brought Elijah was cooked meat, like from a barbecue. Or maybe they brought him road kill. Ick. Except did they have road kill then? Squirrels run over by a speeding chariot? I nearly laughed at myself. I guess God could just create the bread and meat and give that to the ravens.

But what did the ravens think about being messengers? Did other people, like maybe a kid, see a raven carrying food in its beak? Would the kid think that was weird?

So why did God do such a weird thing? Why use ravens? Why not some person? Maybe God did ask people, but no one wanted to, so he asked the ravens. That was an awful thought—no one but the birds would help God.

So all that led up to: Did God tell the crows to help me yesterday? But why? Did God want something from me? Did he want me to do something? But what?

As swiftly as I thought that, another thought flashed by as if on wings. God wanted me to love Kayla and let her know that God loved her too. Obviously something was wrong at her home. So I was here to help her.

But what exactly could I do?

"Hey," yelled Kayla suddenly, and she began to run with Burrito trotting after her. So much for our invisible umbilical cord.

"Hey, what?"

Kayla didn't answer me so I ran after them, eating their dust.

16

X Marks the Spot

A man and a dog stood outside the tent. *Oh great*, I thought. *Now we've got homeless people invading us.* Did they want Onyx, too? Slow rage, like steeping herb tea, spread through me. This stupid, stupid city! I hated it so much!

Kayla slowed and instead of screaming, she called calmly, "Oh, hello, X. What's up?"

Huh?

I caught up and took Burrito's lead line. Kayla was actually smiling. I looked at the man again. He looked familiar.

"Miss Lucy!" shouted Kayla.

One of the ugliest dogs I'd ever seen danced toward her. And I've seen some ugly dogs, including a gnarled, wrinkled bulldog with buck teeth and a missing front leg. His name was Tripod. Miss Lucy was probably a close cousin to Tripod, although she had all four legs.

"She's part mastiff and part boxer." Kayla put out her arms. The bone white beast with a mustard orange patch over one eye lumbered over and licked her face. Kayla hugged her. The man was smiling down at us. He was tall. Maybe over six-six. His skin was the color of coffee and no cream, and he wore red running shorts and a dark blue T-shirt that read, "God Made the Sky Carolina Blue." Suddenly I knew him. He was the youth leader from the church we went to on Sunday.

His smile included all of us, even Burrito. "I haven't seen a donkey in years," he said. "Is he a baby?"

"Almost a year old," I said.

"He's especially handsome. What's his name?"

"Burrito," I said. Burrito pricked his ears at the man as if tuning with antennae.

"How are you today, Kayla?" he asked in a voice that was friendly and low, not false and high like some grown-ups' voices get when talking to kids.

"Oh, okay," she said, her arms still around the ugly dog.

He shifted his glance to me. "Don't tell me," he warned. "Let's see if I can remember your name."

"How do you know her?" demanded Kayla. Jealous? I could have laughed.

"I remember everyone who comes to my church," he said.

"You went to church?" Kayla exclaimed and stared at me. "What for?"

I could have given her the old fallback, "My parents made me," but instead I said, "Because I like God."

Kayla blew out her breath in a half snort, half laugh, and shook her head as if I were a lost cause. Maybe I was.

"It's a good reason," he said. The skin around his eyes crinkled. "Now let's see. Is your name Roberta?"

"He won't remember it," said Kayla triumphantly.

"Patricia, how dare you!" he exclaimed.

"Told you!" Kayla was laughing into Miss Lucy's neck. Burrito jealously sniffed the dog as if he were thinking about snacking on her.

The pastor continued guessing. "Rachel? Robin? Rosa? Rahab?"

"Rahab," yelped Kayla. "She was a prostitute!"

He laughed. "But she is honored in Jesus' family tree."

I stared at them, as if they weren't even talking about me at all. They carried on their own little dialogue, a comedy with serious overtones.

"How do you know about Rahab if you don't go to church?" I was baiting her, but she deserved it.

Kayla shrugged. "I read all kinds of books. Last year I read most of the Koran."

"She's my best scholar," the pastor said proudly.

"I'm not your anything," Kayla snapped. "I don't go to your church."

"Oh, but you do." He held out his arms and gestured to the riverbed, the bike and dirt trails that ran over a hundred miles from mountains to sea. "This is my church, and you're included."

Kayla stuck out her tongue at him and stroked Miss Lucy.

"Reba Castillo," he said quietly as if he knew my name all along. He smiled so that his eyes lit up in their darkness.

"I forget your name," I confessed.

"Malcolm Hills," he said. "You can call me Pastor Malcolm if you want. Most of the kids do."

"I don't call him that," said Kayla.

"What do you call him?" I asked.

"X."

"Huh?" Maybe he was a treasure map; X marks the spot. I could imagine knowing him was like opening a treasure chest—spilling rubies, diamonds, sapphires. Black gold. He seemed like that kind of person.

"X for Malcolm X. That's who he was named after." Then she showed him Onyx and explained how we'd gotten the crow baby. Maybe I could tell him about the crows helping me. He seemed like the kind of grown-up who would believe a kid.

"How long have you known each other?" I asked.

They exchanged thoughtful glances like good friends do when sharing a favorite memory. A stab of envy speared me. *Look who's jealous now.*

"Five years?" said Kayla. "I was in first grade."

"Yep. I'd just come here from North Carolina."

"I was stuck in an oak tree over by the golf course," Kayla explained to me. "I'll show you sometime. It's a great old tree. But X and Miss Lucy got me down."

"What were you doing in the tree?" If it were me, I'd have been trying to rescue a kitten or squirrel.

"Looking around. I could see so far that day. I could see the ocean and the hump of Catalina Island. I even saw the San Gabriel Mountains." She turned to me again. "Why, Reba, I almost could have seen you!"

"She's plain nuts, but she'll do," said Pastor Malcolm. He ruffled her pale hair, and she slugged his shoulder muscle.

"How did you find Kayla's tent?" I asked him. I thought we'd hidden it pretty well.

He winked at me. "I know Kayla better than she thinks. I figured it out."

Kayla made a face. "Miss Lucy probably tracked me here."

At her name, the ugly dog wriggled her tail.

"I'm off," said Pastor Hill. "Got to finish my jog. Glad to see you again, Reba. Behave yourself, Kayla." He and Miss Lucy trotted down the sandy path back up to the levee.

"He's nice," I said.

"He's okay."

"Does he know you sleep here at night?" I asked.

She glared at me. "I never told him." Implication: you better not, either.

"At my old home," I said, trying to choose my words carefully, "they talked to us about abuse."

"You mean like Jantu's cousin?"

"That, too. But I was thinking about you."

"What about me? You think I'm abused? Do I look beat up?" she demanded.

106

Your soul is beat up, I thought. "There are lots of kinds of abuse."

"Like what?"

She was so snarky.

"You tell me," I said.

Stiffly she lifted her tent flap, her lips tight. "I think you better go, Reba."

Fine. I took Burrito's lead line, put Onyx on my shoulder, and stalked away. I didn't even look back. Why did I even bother with her?

17
Not a Nice Trip

At home during dinner around the table Mama complained about Onyx. "That bird! He got out and made messes all over the house."

Darn those stupid boys. If it weren't for them we could keep him on the riverbed, and I wouldn't be getting yelled at. But I didn't tell her any details because if I did, she'd forbid me from going to the riverbed. Then where would I exercise Burrito? The middle of the street? Besides, not going to the riverbed wouldn't keep the boys from bugging us.

"Mama, she likes the bird poop because she has poop for brains," Miguel said.

Andres chortled, waving his taco, bits of meat and tomatoes flying. Francisco stifled a laugh. I glared at Miguel wishing I could turn him into a pile of bird poop.

"If I had some pieces of wood and some wire I could make him a cage," I said.

"I can help you make a cage," said Francisco.

I could hardly lift my gaze to his. I wanted a cage, but I didn't want him to make it. I could do it. I just needed the supplies.

"Where would you get wood and stuff?" I asked through stiff lips.

Francisco neatly folded a tortilla with his big rough fingers. "Easy enough. They are building a new office complex next to La Quinta. I'll ask for scraps."

"That's all the way out to Moreno Valley," Mama protested. "I thought you weren't going out there until next week."

Francisco shrugged. "If Reba needs to build a cage then I go."

Something deep in me stirred, but another part of me, that wary wild beast of me said, *Beware, he's just trying to win you over.*

"Can you get lots of wood?" Andres asked. "I want to build a fort."

Francisco laughed and ruffled his hair. "I try, *m'ijo.*"

Mama's dagger gaze pierced me until I said, "Thank you, Francisco." I looked briefly up at him.

"*De nada,*" he said. *It's nothing.* But his eyes said, *I'd do almost anything for you.*

I looked back down, not wanting to see.

The next day during school the teacher called each of us up to her desk to talk about our in-class essays. We could write about anything we loved. I had written about living in the San Gabriel Mountains.

I stood beside her desk in the front of the room under the tall windows. Sunlight splashed across the desk and onto my paper.

"This is very moving, Reba," she said. "You wrote a good essay. I can see you miss your old home a lot."

My face grew hot. I couldn't answer.

She showed me the many spelling errors and some grammar stuff I did wrong. Then, when she was finished she said again, "I liked your essay very much." She squeezed my hand.

I took my paper and fled down the aisle, my face hot, feeling as prickly as Kayla. Halfway down the aisle a foot shot out. I tripped and fell. Laughter erupted around me.

Ken's face grinned meanly down at me. "I want my crow back," he whispered.

"Never." I hauled myself up.

The teacher was on her feet, marching down the aisle. "What happened?"

Like I'd tattle. I gave Ken my most furious glare, but said, "I just tripped."

She looked as if she didn't believe me. "Are you hurt?"

"No." I returned to my seat. The girl behind me leaned forward and whispered, "I saw stupid Ken stick his foot out. He's a creep."

That I could agree with!

The rest of the day I plotted ways to get even with Ken and those dumb boys. But after each idea of revenge a little voice would add, "Why not pray for them?"

I didn't want to listen to that little voice, so I didn't.

After school, Kayla, Jantu, and I stopped by my house and got Onyx, then cleaned up his messes so Mama wouldn't be mad. Then we walked to the stable, going down the street and through the front way instead of around the dirt road.

Overhead the sky was blue and clear, but to the north the storm clouds gathered and clung to the mountains. I sniffed the air, but I couldn't smell the rain like I usually could back at home. Maybe it had something to do with the thunder and lightning. The air was definitely different here.

Kayla held Onyx on her arm. I didn't tell the teacher, but when Ken tripped me and I fell, I'd hurt my wrist. I had caught myself on both hands, harder on my left wrist, I guess. It didn't hurt real bad, but it had grown puffy like a burro with a strained leg.

"Sue him," said Kayla.

"Yeah, right," I said.

"You have lots of witnesses. We all saw it happen."

"I don't want to sue him," I said. "I want to kill him."

We all laughed.

We walked back to the corrals and stopped laughing. Burrito's corral gate was open, and he was gone.

18
Carrot Bribes

Instantly I knew Ken had stolen him.

Burrito would never leave on his own, even if he could unlatch his gate, which he couldn't. He'd never go willingly with someone he didn't know either. I wondered why the stable dogs weren't around. I hoped Ken hadn't hurt them. Usually they barked their heads off if a stranger appeared.

"Ken wouldn't dare take Burrito to his house because we know where he lives now," said Kayla. "So where would he take him?"

"We smash that Ken and boys," muttered Jantu.

I wanted to smash Ken, too, that was for sure.

"Here's hoofprints." I pointed at a fresh-looking line of small round prints. But I wasn't sure which ones were from this afternoon. I took Burrito out almost every day along this same road. "Let's go up to the corner of the street and see if anyone saw a burro. He sort of stands out."

Near the corner a couple of kids played on their dirt front lawn. They tossed an almost flat red plastic ball.

"Did you see anyone with a donkey?" asked Kayla.

The kids, two little boys, drew together, big eyed, silent. I repeated the question in Spanish. They relaxed and one jabbered about the toy that walked.

"He's no toy," I said.

One of the boys picked up a piece of carrot from the street. "The boy was giving him this," he said.

Luring Burrito out with carrots, his one weakness. "Which way did they go?" I asked.

The boys pointed down Seventeenth Street, away from the riverbed.

That surprised me. "*Gracias!*"

We ran down the street. Two blocks down in front of three-story, pink-colored apartments was a small pile of burro poop. We kept running.

Kayla held her right side. "I can't run anymore," she gasped and slowed. "Go on. There's a park near here. I bet they went there."

"Lazy," teased Jantu.

But that wasn't like Kayla. I didn't stop to ask her about it, though. Time for that later. Jantu and I just kept running. A small road sign read: Eastside Park. We turned down the street.

A crowd of mostly kids, a few adults, were gathered near a basketball court. I ran harder. Jantu pounded after me.

In the center of the crowd, Ken, Jesse, Pepe, and Thay stood with my burro. They wore uncertain looks on their faces as many hands reached out to stroke the burro. Burrito was busy munching.

I elbowed my way through the crowd. "Excuse me, excuse me, that's my burro."

People shifted aside and I shoved in. The crowd wanting to see Burrito had stopped the boys.

Ken saw me first and shouted, "She stole my donkey!"

I was so stunned I just stood there stupidly.

Jantu barreled after me, hollering, "Not true! Not true! These boys thieves!"

The crowd murmured and a few kids laughed. Burrito chomped a carrot, and orange drool dribbled down his chin. He pricked his ears at me, but kept eating. The pig.

Ken said loudly, "We need to get going now." He tugged at the lead line. When Burrito didn't budge, Jesse dangled a carrot before his nose. Right on cue, Burrito stuck his nose toward the carrot, and began walking behind Ken.

"Burrito," I called, trying to keep my voice calm. "Come here now."

He paused, chewing, and looked back over his shoulder. Ken pulled at the lead line, but Burrito stood still. Relief washed over me. He was a little donkey, but stronger than Ken. If he didn't want to cooperate

114

there was no way Ken or even all four boys could drag him very far.

"Come on, Burrito," I said again, and he took a couple of steps toward me.

Jesse held another carrot under his nose, and he turned to grab the carrot. But as he reached for it, Jesse held it in front until Burrito walked several yards away with Ken. Then Burrito gobbled down the carrot. I was about to lose to Burrito's stomach!

I could just imagine myself in court trying to prove Burrito was mine. He wasn't branded and he wasn't registered or anything. I couldn't prove with paperwork that he was mine. Would the judge believe me? Surely a judge would believe Mama and the lady who boarded him, wouldn't he?

I called Burrito again. "Let's go home, Burrito, come on."

He tugged toward me, but Ken yanked back. "Give him another carrot," Ken hissed.

Jesse held up an empty plastic bag. "All gone."

Ken stamped his foot.

I had them now! "Burrito. Home," I said, turning my back and walking away.

The crowd parted. Ken and Jesse yelled Burrito's name. Sounds of grunting and struggles rose behind me. I grinned and resisted the temptation to turn around. Jantu stood in front of me, facing the turmoil. She smiled and gave me the thumbs-up sign.

The crowd was laughing and shouting. As I reached the edge of the park, the familiar tattoo of hooves rattled behind me. A soft nose rested on my shoulder.

"Burrito." I threw my arms around his neck and kissed his still damp, carrot orange nose.

That night at home I thought about bringing Burrito to our yard, but how would I explain it to Mama? It all went back to if I told her she'd forbid me to go to the riverbed. I thought about locking Burrito's stall, but that was sort of dangerous; in case of an emergency, like a fire, someone wouldn't be able to release him.

As I thought more about it I had the feeling Ken wouldn't take him again. Sure, he could get more carrots, but Burrito could only eat so many. Eventually the burro would refuse to cooperate. I wondered where Ken thought he'd keep Burrito anyhow.

That afternoon, after I'd returned Burrito to his corral, I'd told the owner of the stable that some boys were hanging around bothering my burro. I managed to hint that they could pester the horses, too. She apologized and told me she had taken the stable dogs that afternoon to the vet for their shots. The dogs were back now. So if Ken did try to come again, the dogs would probably scare him off. At least they'd alert the owner.

After dinner I turned on my boom box to the rock station KLOS, and I worked on my homework: reading a dumb short story in English, and two chapters of American history (no Spanish or Mexican people were mentioned as if the whole world were run by only whites), then doing twenty math equations. Yuck-o.

Mama knocked, and Onyx squawked as she came in. She dumped a rumpled load of clean jeans and shirts on my bed. I'd forgotten them outside on the clothesline.

"The news says rain tonight. I didn't think you wanted them washed again."

"I forgot about them. Thanks, Mama."

"You got an umbrella to take to school tomorrow? Remember, Francisco and I have to leave early in the morning for Moreno Valley. He says he'll get the wood and things for the cage." She glared at Onyx as if it were his fault. Onyx just preened a wing as he sat on his makeshift perch over piles of newspapers.

"I got an umbrella," I said.

"Be careful going to school. You know how people drive so crazy in the rain." She kissed my forehead. In southern California people drove on wet streets like burros skidding in their new metal shoes.

"Si, Mama." I paused a moment and added, "Tell Francisco thanks."

"Tell him yourself." She left.

I put my elbows on the windowsill and nuzzled aside the old, soft curtains from my bedroom at the pack station. We'd had to shorten them. Windows are smaller in the city, I guess. Not as much to look at.

The wind sang through the roof as I finally finished my homework and went to bed.

19
Downpour

A thud. A sharp clink against the window next to my bed. I sat up in bed.

I was gasping with fear while the heavy darkness pressed down. Outside the wind called. Had the wind awakened me? Was it Andres? Having a nightmare?

Slowly I slid from the warm covers. My blankets were woven out of alpaca wool by a relative; they were thick and deep and colored dark as night.

Another clink against the glass pane. Something had definitely hit my window, square and neat. Not a random eucalyptus bud, but singular and loud. I crouched on the floor, then crawled to the window. My curtains lay in deep folds of green and blue. The streetlight glowed around the edges.

I peeked between the sill and the bottom edge of the curtain ruffle. What was out there? A monster?

Right, Reba. Like a monster would toss a rock against my windowpane to alert me that he was there.

The wind was driving like it does before unleashing rain. Leaves and loose papers rolled down the street, sometimes hesitating for a moment, only to be torn loose from whatever had caught them, and rippled along the wind streams.

A movement caught my eye and for a fraction of a second my heart caught and pounded furiously against my ribs. Not a monster. A person motion. Sean? My friend from the mountains? How could he be here at night outside my window? No, a robber. One of those stupid boys trying to steal Onyx.

I eased up the window. Ken came forward readily.

"Man, you sleep like you're dead," he whispered.

"Yeah and I'm glad to see you, too," I hissed. "Which of my animals are you trying to steal this time?"

"Hey, I'm sorry about that."

"Yeah, right."

"We've got to get Kayla out," he said.

I stared at him a minute, trying to decide if he was truly crazy. "Huh?" I finally said.

"Don't be stupid. We have to get her out. Come on." The wind thundered behind him, and something in the dark cracked like a gunshot.

"Okay, I'll try not to be stupid." I glanced over my shoulder at my digital clock: 2:14 a.m. "About twelve hours ago you stole my burro, and now you're at my house in the middle of the night. Give me a clue, Ken."

I wondered if I should go wake Mama and Francisco. This whole thing was a huge pain.

Ken put his face close to the dirty screen and said in a steady voice: "Kayla sleeps in the riverbed. It's starting to rain. It's raining north of here. Do you know what happens to this riverbed when it rains?"

My anger shredded as if a laser had pierced it. The memory of a flash flood in a canyon in the San Gabriels roared through my brain. "I'll be right out," I said.

I shoved the window shut, changed quickly into jeans and a jacket, opened the window again, pushed out the screen, and hopped out the window into the backyard.

The air was moist, heavy, and the wind rushed through our little yard. We crept around the house and eased open the side gate, right under Mama's window. Please God, don't let them hear me. I couldn't imagine trying to explain to Mama or Francisco what I was doing at two in the morning sneaking outside with a boy. They wouldn't understand. Or would they? For a moment I paused. Maybe I should get their help.

The wind whipped around the front of the house, and with it cold drops of rain burst over us. No time to try to explain.

"How do you know Kayla is there tonight?" I called.

The wind and rain tossed my words down the street. He started jogging along the damp sidewalk. I ran after him, yelling my question in his ear.

"Her mom works tonight," he shouted back.

So he at least knew what I knew about her. I remember her saying she'd known Ken since first grade. Sudden insight struck me. Did Ken like Kayla? Maybe all this stealing animals and stuff was to get her attention?

I groaned to myself. My mind skiddered up and down, thinking of the riverbed, of Kayla, of Ken and the guys. I wondered how fast the riverbed would fill. The rain transformed from individual drops to pelting rivulets. Typical, hard driving California rain. Especially with rain up the river, the riverbed would fill in minutes, not hours.

Ken turned down the stable road which was rapidly growing muddy.

"Why are you going here?" I shouted and leaped a two-foot-wide puddle.

"Get your donkey and a rope. We might need it!"

I realized that was a good idea.

We fled into the barn of the Tennessee Walking horses. One whinnied. In the tack room, which thankfully wasn't locked, I grabbed a couple of longe lines, long nylon webbing used to exercise horses. Then at the pipe corrals, I snatched Burrito's halter and lead line from the hook outside the gate.

Ken's hair was plastered to his head like a horse's forelock. I tossed him the two longe lines and got Burrito.

Burrito seemed to know something was up and waited patiently at the gate, holding very still to be haltered. Could he know what we were to do?

When I threw open his gate, he immediately trotted out, and we ran back down the road. The puddle, when I jumped it again, was nearly twice as wide.

The streets were shiny and wet, nearly empty. We reached the riverbed fast. On the levee, the only lights were from Jantu's apartment complex, glinting into the wild night and shining off a rushing darkness in the riverbed.

"Look at the water!" Ken hollered.

I was looking. And I was scared.

20

The Call
of the
Water

Water surged completely across the riverbed. I couldn't tell how deep it was. Already, broken tree limbs, wooden boards, metal gutters, and other debris were jetting past in the brown frothing water. I stared hard where Kayla's camp should have been. In the blasting rain and darkness I had trouble seeing any details unless the reflected lights rimmed an object, like bedsprings coursing along. Yet in an occasional pause in the rain, the center of the riverbed showed whitish, like a peeled egg. The sand bar of Kayla's camp.

"She has to be gone already," Ken said. His unspoken words were, "She's washed away."

Burrito leaned against me and snuffled, ears upright. Uncle Hector had told me burros could track as well as any dog and that, even though many people didn't think it was possible, scents could be tracked through water. I'd seen Uncle Hector's two hunting dogs follow a scent once in the San Gabriel River.

"Do you smell Kayla?" I asked softly. "Is she out there?" Burrito pressed forward, his ears pricked toward her camp.

"We better go back and get help," said Ken.

But I knew that by the time we ran to the nearest phone and called for help, the river could wash away the sand spit and Kayla with it. If she was there.

Burrito took another step forward. Normally he didn't like water, getting wet. Maybe because he was already soaked from the rain, he was willing to go on.

"Burrito thinks she's still here," I said. I wasn't certain of that, but I wasn't willing to assume she was safely away. How would I feel if her body was found downstream?

He stared at me, then at the burro. "What should we do?"

I handed him the end of the longe line. "I'll tie this around me. Let's tie the end to—" I paused looking behind us. Nothing was close enough.

"Tie it to Burrito," said Ken.

"He isn't really trained to pull." But what else could I do? Ken probably couldn't hold me if the river snatched me; its force was so great.

I tied a heart hitch around Burrito, a circle of rope around his belly so the rope fed out between his forelegs. Then I tied the other end around my waist.

"Here's the plan," I said rapidly. "Stand here with Burrito and play out the longe line. Keep it taut, okay? There's no use both of us going into the river." *And both of us drowning*, I thought.

Ken started to shake his head.

"Do you suppose Kayla would go with you?" I said angrily. "After all you've done?"

He stopped shaking his head.

"I'm going." I took a deep breath and nearly choked on rain water. My canvas tennis shoes hit the icy water. All my formed thoughts tumbled like broken twigs in a swift current.

Jump into cold water fast. The old childhood saying bobbed to the surface of my racing thoughts. I walked slowly down the steep side, holding the taut rope for balance.

My feet stepped free of the cement as the water whirled up to my thighs, knocking me off my feet. Terror zinged through me. In my hands the rope burned like the icy water on my legs. I had hardly gulped out, "Help, Lord," when over the rush of water came the sound of crows.

Crows dark as the storm. Voices loud as the storm.

Suddenly my fear receded. I understood. The Lord was sending my fears to the crows so they could fly them away.

I took a new grip on the rope and walked farther out into the angry river. Choppy waves flung themselves up to my waist. The low furious force dragged at me, but I hung on to the rope, praying Ken would keep it taut.

Sloshing step by step over the shifting bottom of the river, I made my way to the sand bar. Something jabbed into my ankle, and pain jolted up my leg. I think I screamed, but the wind snatched all sound into a constant river shriek.

Then I saw the tent, a deflated, crumpled ball tangled in the remaining thicket.

I knew better than to rush and risk tripping. If I fell the river would take me away. Far away.

I started to call Kayla's name when a sudden burst of heavier rain poured down on me. It was like the time Miguel had climbed up on the burro barn's roof and poured a bucket of water over my head as I walked by. Only this wasn't one bucket, but bucket after bucket.

I stood, gasping. A thousand miles away, Burrito brayed, mournful as a coyote's howl.

When the rain let up a fraction, I moved higher onto the sandbar.

"Kayla?" I called. My fingers touched the plastic hump of the tent. It moved, rippling in the wind as if alive.

"Are you stupid or what?" Kayla appeared from under the tent. Her pale hair streamed and blurred into the rain. She was hunched over as if the pressure of the rain were holding her down.

"I was about to ask you the same question," I said. "Let's get out of here."

"I can't," she said flatly.

"Why not?"

"I hurt too much. I can hardly stand up."

"What's wrong?" Had a large branch or something struck her?

"I don't know," she said. "I feel like someone is stabbing my side."

I had to get her across the water somehow. "Come on," I said. "I'll help you." I put my arm around her shoulders. Still hunched over, she let me guide her through the soggy sand.

"How did you know I was here?" she asked through clenched teeth.

"Ken came to my house and woke me up."

"Ken!" She gave a harsh laugh.

Just before we started into the water I untied the longe line and retied it under her arms. She wouldn't let me even touch her side.

"Now," I said and stepped in.

The current snatched at us. My feet slipped, and I nearly went down. Kayla screamed, whether in fear or pain or both I didn't know. But I did know the water was calling me, and I had better get us out fast.

21
Darkness Shot With Light

Now, how to get Kayla up the steep side. Her hand slipped in mine so we gripped our fingers around each other's wrists until our joints cracked.

Please help us, God, I prayed.

Ken appeared on the edge of the levee. I could scream all I wanted and he'd never hear me. I just pointed at Kayla, then pointed up at him, hoping he'd get the idea.

The churning water continued to rise. Up the levee the longe line was tightening. I kept remembering what Francisco had said the other night about the last rains. A flood control worker had been knocked down; he drowned in less than four feet of rushing water.

I helped steady Kayla as she began climbing the steep cement wall. She held her side and that made her even more unsteady. About halfway up, her feet slipped out from under her, and she kicked me as she flailed. The rope held her, but I slid back down into the channel with a chilling splash.

The water was easily three feet deep. As I splashed back into it, my feet and hands slipped even more in the slick mud. I tried to gain my balance when my ankle cracked against something hard, and I fell completely in. Then the water took me.

Half in a daze, I opened my eyes as a huge sucking noise exploded behind me. The wooden golf course bridge splintered down from its frame. Timbers cracked and hit the river. Pieces of the bridge gained on me as the current swirled us along. I had to get out! If the water didn't do me in, the wooden bridge would.

But I couldn't swim hard enough to break the grip of the current. Besides, I was exhausted and so cold that my fingers felt gone. I thought I heard Kayla screaming, but then all sound was cut off except the roaring of the water.

Think hard, Reba. You've gotten yourself out of trouble before. But my mind was sluggish. All I could think of was: *Help me, God*.

A nasty little voice said back, You've used your God card too many times. It's expired.

No, God doesn't work like that. That thought was clear.

One of the bridge boards seemed caught on something and wasn't moving as fast as I was. As I whirled by, I grabbed it. I clung to it like a life ring, and it held me up.

Suddenly a surge of water broke over me like a wave. I went under, still holding the board. I bobbed back up, sputtering, choking, thankful I was still clinging to the board.

The rainfall was heavy and blocked the light until finally a current of pure darkness closed around me. I knew what that meant. No circle of crows would save me this time. My brain shifted away from words.

The water's tremendous weight pushed me deeper. My arms and legs were so heavy, so cold, like when I'd plunge into the San Gabriel Mountain streams on a hot summer day. I was freezing. But my lungs were on fire.

Something hard crashed into me, and flashes of light struck through my darkness. Air. I needed air. I struggled. Weeds broke apart under my feet. My head broke the surface of the flailing river, and air rushed into my burning lungs, cooling them.

Then something grabbed me. I'd be pulled down again! I struggled, but it didn't let go. I was dragged up and out of the sucking water, out of the clinging weeds and junk. I let go of the board. It whirled away in the water. My eyes wouldn't open, but I could see through my eyelids.

Cool, I thought, words coming back into my brain. Then circles of light drenched through my eyelids. The light hurt so much that I wanted the darkness to carry me away again. So it did.

When I finally opened my eyes, the dark remained, but it was broken by jagged spears of light. Something warm pressed around me and was moving me, but not through water. I wiggled my toes. My shoes and socks were gone, and my bare toes felt encased in ice.

The rushing noise was the too-familiar sound of the river running. The river had taken me, yet it had released me. I struggled and someone said, "It's all right, Reba." Francisco. I was in Francisco's arms. Then we were climbing, leaving the angry water behind.

"Here she is!" shouted Francisco as he crested the levee. How did he know I'd be here?

My lips were cold and hard to move. I forced out the words, "Is Kayla all right?"

"The blonde girl?" He held me tight and for once I didn't mind his closeness. "They're on their way to the hospital. Something about appendicitis." Of course. That was why her side hurt.

Light flooded us, and a couple of firemen in brilliant yellow slickers appeared. One took Francisco's arm, helping him. "Anyone else out there with you?" one asked me.

"Is Ken with you?" I asked. "And Burrito?"

"The white boy," said Francisco, "and my daughter's burro." The fireman nodded. "One of the cops is escorting the boy home." I hoped he wouldn't be in trouble.

"Burro's fine," said the fireman helping Francisco. I relaxed in Francisco's arms, thinking, *He called me his daughter.*

"Was another girl with you?" asked the fireman. "One with a heavy Vietnamese or something accent?"

"Jantu? I never saw her here," I said.

"She's the one who called us out," he said.

A third fireman appeared and corrected him, "That girl called from her home. Said she saw her friends down in the riverbed."

Jantu and her eagle eyes.

"I think I can walk," I said.

Francisco put me down and I nearly collapsed, but managed with his help to stagger to the ambulance. The paramedic gave me the once over and decided I could go on home. As my fingers and toes came back to life they burned and hurt like a fury.

"You're lucky," said one paramedic. "If your father hadn't pulled you out when he did you'd be a goner."

There it was again. My father. Francisco had brought dry, warm clothes for me, and I changed into them. I knew luck wasn't what helped me.

"Let's go," said Francisco. "Your mama's frantic. I made her stay at the house with the boys."

I smiled, imagining Mama. She thought she could protect me from everything by her presence.

"I've got the car up on the bridge," he said.

"But Burrito," I protested. "I have to take him home."

One of the firemen offered to walk my burro back.

"But he needs to be rubbed down," I said.

"I've worked with horses," said the fireman. "I can take care of him." I explained how to get to the stable.

Francisco helped me as we hiked up to our car, which was parked near a fire truck and two squad cars, their emergency lights flashing. I sank into the front seat, and Francisco draped a blanket over me.

"How did you know where I was?" I asked him as he pulled away from the railing.

"A father makes it his business to know," he said, and I fell asleep before we even got home.

22
Sunlight Again

"You have to tell me what happened," said Jantu. "I couldn't see much."

It was three days later, and Jantu and I were sitting on a bench in the small park near CHOC, the Children's Hospital. We had walked over after school to see Kayla, and we were waiting for Ken to join us.

I told her everything I could remember. While I was in the water things seemed unreal, like a strange, vivid dream. But I had the bruises and cuts to prove I'd really been there.

Jantu nodded throughout my story. "Good your stepfather help you," she said.

That had been good. In fact, Francisco had saved my life.

"But how did you know to call 911?" I blinked at her in the bright sunlight.

"I watch out the window. My sister sleep light. I want to help Kayla. I know Kayla be down there. Then I see movement on the levee. I see Burrito. So I creep to phone in kitchen and call 911 for emergency, just like they say on television."

Ken rode up on his bike. "Let's go see Kayla." He locked his bike, and the three of us walked into the hospital. It was a children's hospital, so bright colored and not very hospital-like in looks. But it was still creepy.

"How come you no walk with us?" asked Jantu as we rode the elevator to the fourth floor. "You still better than us?"

Ken's eyes sparkled. He didn't answer except to unzip his jacket. Onyx was tucked into his shirt. The crow blinked at us as if we'd awakened him. Jantu and I tried not to laugh, but we couldn't help it. Ken zipped his jacket back up, hiding the crow as the elevator doors whooshed open. A few people gave us annoyed glares as we walked down the hall, giggling, but some seemed glad to see laughter.

As we approached Kayla's room, we fell silent. Jantu pushed me and Ken fell in behind her, so I walked in first.

Kayla was sitting up, grinning. "I heard you guys laughing." That broke us all up. Then, after glancing around for nurses, Ken showed Kayla the stowaway in his shirt.

She looked happier than I'd ever seen her look before. One of her arms had an IV tube stuck into it, and she let Onyx hop onto the other arm. He gargled joyously at her.

"Don't let him poop on your incision," I said, and that set us all off laughing again.

"It hurts to laugh," said Kayla, gasping, and laughing anyway.

Jantu pointed at a plant arrangement on the shelf. "Who give you that?"

"X and his wife. They came to see me," said Kayla. "He and his wife are trying to get me as a foster kid. My stepfather was arrested," she added quietly.

I didn't know what to say to that, when Jantu, her face awestruck, said, "This look like mai-ya-rah." She pointed at one of the plants.

"Huh?" said Kayla.

"In Khmer," Jantu explained, "we have a plant, like this, what do you call it?"

"A fern," said Kayla.

"Fern. If you touch, it curl up. Later it opens and is stronger. I always say to myself I be like mai-ya-rah. No matter what happens I come back stronger."

"I like that," said Kayla. "I want to be that way, too." I think we all did.

A nurse bustled in. "How are you feeling, Kayla? Any pain? Nice your friends are here." Then she gave a low shriek.

We went into laughter again, and Ken took Onyx back under his jacket.

Once the nurse got over her surprise, she was smiling, but she still said, "You need to take that animal out now."

So we said good-bye and left. We didn't want to get Kayla in trouble. As if she needed more trouble.

Outside the sun was shining as if it hadn't rained a drop in years. Ken took Onyx out and put him on his handlebars.

"Francisco's going to build a cage this weekend," I said.

"I'll bring him over on Sunday," said Ken.

"In the afternoon," I reminded him. "Because of church." Something made me look up and in one of the windows someone was waving. "There's Kayla," I exclaimed.

We all waved madly, the sunlight falling in a blaze of gold around us.

Reba Novels

The Reba novel series offers the best in reading entertainment for the middle schooler. Well-crafted writing, realistic characters, and exciting situations help readers test and find true their own Christian beliefs.

The Bounty Hunter (#1)
0-310-54351-7
$5.99

When Reba and her friend Sean rescue an unusual creature from a bounty hunter in the wild San Gabriel mountains, Reba learns the power of faith—and the strength of love.

The Runaways (#2)
0-310-54361-4
$5.99

Reba's mother is remarrying—and Reba can't stand her new stepfather. Her solution? Running away to a secret network of caves in the mountains, safe from discovery by her family. Then God puts Reba through her darkest trial yet, and she finds out just how much her family means to her.

Kayla's Secret (#3)
0-310-43351-7
$5.99

New friends and adventure await Reba when she moves to the city. When Reba helps save a baby crow from neighborhood boys, she becomes friends with Jantu and Kayla. But danger threatens in the middle of the night when a flash flood threatens to sweep Kayla away. Can Reba save her without being drowned herself?

Lost on Catalina Island (#4)
0-310-43761-X
$5.99

Clashing personalities, misplaced maps, and a ruined two-way radio turn a hike on a desert island into a trial of endurance for Reba and her three teammates. But difficulty turns to disaster when one of the kids is bitten by a rattlesnake. Suddenly, every minute counts in a desperate race against time to save his life.

Marian Flandrick Bray's books are available at fine bookstores everywhere.

ZondervanPublishingHouse
Grand Rapids, Michigan
http://www.zondervan.com

America Online
AOL Keyword:zon

A Division of HarperCollinsPublishers